Twisted Souls

Amanda Penn

This is a work of fiction. Similarities to real people, places, or events are entirely coincidental.

TWISTED SOULS

First edition. August 9, 2024.

Copyright © 2024 Amanda Penn.

ISBN: 979-8224630394

Written by Amanda Penn.

I want to thank the silent rock stars of the writing world. To my Alpha readers, Megan, Taylee and Joey Lyn and my editor, Raven. I adore you all. Thank you for rooting me on from the beginning.

Before Reading this please read. This book contains many subjects that may be disturbing. Your mental health matters. So, if any of these subjects are disturbing for you, please do not continue.

-Abusive relationships -Hospitalization -Reapers

-Alcohol -Kidnapping -Ghosts

-Alcoholism -Loss of parents -The afterlife

-Anxiety - Murder

-Assault -Pedophilia

-Attempted murder -Physical abuse

-Attempted rape -Poisoning

-Blood -Profanity

-Bones -Prostitution

-Bullying -PTSD

-Car accident -Rape

-Child abuse -Satan/The Devil

-Death -Self-harm

-Demons -Sexism

-Depression -Sexual abuse

-Drugs -Sexual assault

-Drug addiction -Sexual Harassment

-Emesis -Sex slavery

-Emotional abuse -Slut shaming

- Gore -Suicide

-Gun violence -Torture

-Hallucinations -Violence

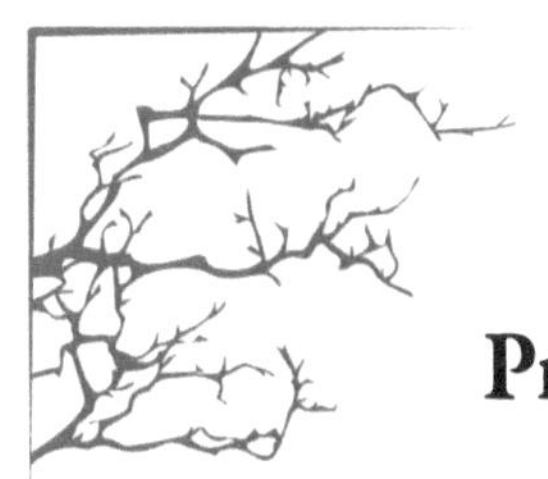

Prologue/ Hunter

I HAVE HEARD THROUGHOUT my life that choices define you, shape you, and make you who you are. I didn't fully grasp that concept until I was standing at a crossroads, trying to choose which path to take. Left or right? My emotions were rolling through me like thunder, and I understood even before I took a step whatever choice I made would be life-altering, life-changing, and very well could be life-ending.

Sometimes, the little voice that should warn me would go ignored because there was something else, or someone else, beckoning me to go down the path that anyone else would have avoided. It is thick with darkened trees and vines covering the path, warning me. Hell, there's even a big warning sign that hangs from a single chain swaying in the wind telling me not to go. During the times I didn't listen to the warnings, I would have still taken that step and then, another and another until I was in the thick of the forest about to be eaten alive.

With my sister, Desi's first tear, I could sense my feet point toward that path and with each word that tumbled from her lips, I took another step into that forest.

"Hunter," she sobbed while she lay on her bed, curled into a ball, her dark hair sticking to her face from the tears she had cried for the last two hours. My hands curled into fists at my side as I tried to control my breathing. She whispered, "I'm sorry."

I forced my thickened breath through my nose and out of my mouth to calm my racing heart, blinking to force away my thoughts, but they kept coming.

She's eleven.

She's a child.
An innocent child.
What kind of monster would touch a child?

The last thought made me flinch because I understood what kind of monster would. He wore a human mask well. Hell, he even wore a suit and had a prominent job... The mayor of the fucking town, for god's sake. He ran Josephine Bay, Georgia, giving him complete access to his victims.

My stomach rolled as I bent forward and kissed Desi's cheek, my own tears threatening to come when she flinched away from me. The anger still coursed through my veins, hot as lava, but I didn't want her to think this was her fault.

"There is nothing to be sorry for," I said, lowering my voice to a whisper so I wouldn't disturb my parents who were crying in the living room because they had allowed the monster in, believing in his humanity because of the pretty mask. They were packing, throwing things in boxes, trying to leave this place for Desi's sake, but I refused to go.

"But I—"

"No, Desi," I said, my brows furrowing. "None of this is your fault. It's *his*."

I gritted my teeth. My words held no meaning to her though. Her eyes still darkened in a way that would follow her for the rest of her life, eating away her soul a piece at a time. Only relief from the danger would soften the blow, and I was going to make sure that relief came.

"I love you," I said, straightening. "No matter what has happened, I love you just as much as I always have."

"I love you too," she said, her eyes closing in relief. "I'm tired, Hunter... So tired."

"Close your eyes until mom and dad come for you," I said, raising my chin. "Get some sleep."

She nodded, her eyes drooping closed. When her breathing evened out, I stared at her, so small in her bed, taking her in for the last time.

As I made my way to the monster's house, I looked up at the sky, surprised at its beauty in all this darkness. The moment his house came into view, I sensed a shift in me which told me to glance around, take everything in, pull each image into my soul before choosing the path.

Left or right? Life or death? I raised my chin and took another step into that forest, but now I was lost in it. Though I will never doubt facing the monster was the right decision, I will regret the way he devoured me.

Because in retrospect, even while I stepped over the threshold into his house, I knew... I knew this was the night I was going to die.

Chapter One/ Hunter

I SUPPOSE NO ONE REALLY knows when their deaths are going to come, but the moment I entered the home office of Jim Harris, I sensed the breath of death touching the back of my neck, raising the dark hair there. His smile was cocky and sure when he reached out his hand to me, expecting me to shake it like I always had. Instead, I stared at it like it was a snake, poised to bite me.

"Hunter," he said in that false pleasant voice, raising his dark brow. His smile grew when I ignored his hand. He glanced at it and shrugged before pulling it away. "I assume this isn't a friendly chat."

Almost as if they realized the danger I presented, two men dressed in black suits flanked me, their muscled arms crossed in front of them, awaiting instructions from their boss. I guess I should have realized I was outnumbered, but at that moment, I didn't care.

"You touched my sister, you sick son of a bitch!" I spat out and though the smile slipped from his face and his brown eyes darkened as he regarded me, he was calm... Nothing about him seemed nervous. Instead, he straightened, more confident than ever.

"And you believe her?" he asked, raising one of his black, bushy eyebrows. I wanted to hit him so much I envisioned it perfectly, but the moment I made the move, his goons were on me, grabbing my arms, pressing their fingertips into the muscles of my biceps, bruising the bones.

The bastard chuckled. "You know I was going to try to convince you she was lying," Jim said, walking behind his desk and opening his drawer. My eyes widened when he pulled out a handgun. "You should have at least pretended you believed me, and I wouldn't have to do this."

"Why would I believe you over my sister?" I asked, keeping my eyes on the gun, held loosely by his side. My heart picked up speed as if trying to put in a few more beats before the end came.

"It's too late to ask that question," he said, tilting his head to study me, his dark eyes soulless and gleaming. He was enjoying this. "But I want you to know, she cried... She cried a lot."

My heart shattered as I began to struggle. If I was going to die, I wanted to hurt him before I did, but his men held me so tightly, I was unable to move.

He raised the gun and while I stared down the tunnel of the barrel, everything was clear. I was going to die and stupidly for thinking I could confront this man and break his jaw before telling the news outlets around the city exactly what kind of person the people had voted for. I had let my anger rule my actions.

The gun went off with a deafening bang. Oddly, I felt no pain when it entered my head. As the light dimmed on my life, Jim's voice fell around me one last time.

"Fetch Shayla Bell," he said, his voice too calm for someone who had just committed a murder. "I want her to see what she caused."

My mind latched onto the girl's name as I drifted away. *Shayla Bell.*

I EXPECTED A TUNNEL of light, but it never came. Instead, a thick oily darkness surrounded me while my soul was pulled through the abyss. A dim light moved over the area in front of me like a light on a dark stage. A dark, shadowed figure stood in front of me, his face completely covered. He regarded me for a moment. A long sigh escaped from the dark void where his face should have been.

My mother's voice surrounded me, falling around me like gentle rain. For a second, I saw her counting down her rosary, rubbing each bead between her fingers. I was shaken with the knowledge she would never know what had become of me.

"You died defending the innocent," a rough, aged voice spoke from the shadowed place beneath the hood. "You deserve justice."

"Fetch Shayla Bell," Jim's voice echoed around me again and again. I latched onto her name. A cry I did not recognize echoed through the darkness, but it ripped at my soul. My name fell around me. I tilted my head, hearing a heartbeat, but it faded, dissolving into the surrounding void.

"You are bound to that name," that rough, aged voice said. "Perhaps, the owner will lead you to the justice you seek."

I would have spoken, begged for that chance to make things even... To make things right, but I couldn't. White light moved around me, brightening more and more, weaving my soul into the shape of my body as it had been right before the bullet had pierced my brain.

"You can speak now, Hunter," the voice said. "But I ask this question; do you want justice?"

"I do," I answered, anger as potent as poison sliding through my voice.

Shayla Bell's name fell around me once more, crashing like glass on my conscience. Jim's voice fell like shards around me again. "Fetch Shayla Bell. I want her to see what she caused."

She was the reason I died. I didn't know why, but she was the reason Jim found Desi. She was the reason for it all. I would deal with her first and then Jim. They would die.

"Very well," the cloaked man said sharply. "She will lead you to it, but remember, the path to things that may be justified is dark and twisted. It is a journey of many forks and turns. Be sure what you choose to do is the right thing, so it doesn't darken your soul."

Then, I fell to earth. When I opened my eyes, I found the green eyes of a beautiful girl named Shayla Bell. Though I should have been mesmerized by her, I wasn't. Instead, I experienced only rage. She was the girl who had allowed my sister to be harmed. She was the one who had caused me to die.

SHE WASN'T ABLE TO see me... And I couldn't touch her. I was a fucking ghost. It was a sick trick... One that only enraged me more as I followed her throughout her day.

As I studied her, I realized I recognized her from somewhere, but my memory couldn't place her. It was driving me insane. I followed her from the street where I had been deposited in front of her to a building that made my blood run cold... The community center where Desi took art classes.

"No," I whispered because I realized this was where Shayla had met her, exposing her to Jim.

I trailed her inside, watching as her long black hair swayed, wishing I could jerk her back by it and make her fall to the floor.

She moved toward the desk where an elderly woman sat with a kind smile sliding over her face.

"Hi, Mrs. Graham," Shayla said in a deceptively gentle voice, further convincing the sweet lady before her that she was innocent and kind.

"Shayla," she said, coming around the desk to hug her. I narrowed my eyes, sure I would be nauseated at her act of kindness, if I were still alive.

"I came to tell you that I won't be volunteering anymore," Shayla said, her voice dripping with sadness. "I-I have too many obligations outside of the community center."

Mrs. Graham's expression drooped. "I'm sorry to hear that, dear," she said as Shayla sighed, her eyes filled with melancholy.

"I am sorry to have to do it," Shayla whispered, seeming on the verge of tears.

Mrs. Graham nodded. "It's fine, dear," she patted her shoulder with one aged hand. "If you ever want to return, your space will still be here."

A small child came out of the room and Mrs. Graham excused herself. Shayla moved toward a cork board with pictures pinned to it. Her eyes moved over it until she reached forward to touch one particular picture near the center. My eyes narrowed as anger pulsed through me. I stared at the image of Desi with Shayla's arm thrown over her shoulders. Both were grinning at the camera.

Quickly, she unpinned it and put it into the purse slung over her shoulder before straightening and leaving the building. As she stepped onto the sidewalk, a familiar voice called her name.

"Remembering your time with Desi?" Jim asked from behind her. His voice alone caused something to break inside of me as I turned to take in my murderer's face. He was grinning as he moved toward her with the smug assurance of someone who knew they would never face consequences for any evil deed committed.

She stiffened, turning toward him, narrowing her eyes. "What are you doing here?" she asked, gritting her teeth.

"Just making sure you remember where you are supposed to be tonight," he said, keeping that smug smile on his face.

"Of course, I do," she said, curling her lip. "I wouldn't want more consequences for my mistakes."

Jim moved closer. "Neither do I," he said, staring into her eyes. "If you need reminding of those consequences, perhaps you should go to the beach and stare out over the waves. Maybe the serenity there will help show you the gravity of those mistakes."

"I will be at your house tonight," Shayla said, her voice cold and emotionless.

As Jim turned to leave her, rage built in me to such a great degree that I punched through the air, my fist going through Shayla's cheek. She shivered as an image of Desi's tear-streaked face slid through my mind. Somehow, I had accessed her memory. I narrowed my eyes at the girl in front of me, realizing that she had been there when Desi was hurt. She had watched the whole damn thing.

Chapter Two/ Shayla

I HAVE ONE MEMORY THAT is bright. It's one of those memories that catches up to me when there is a sepia-tinted atmosphere in the air. There's something nostalgic about the way the wind blows and the leaves crackle as they move across the concrete sidewalks. There is even something to the scent that wraps around me, drifting up my nose and reminding me of the precise scent of baking cookies. It is as if I'm walking in a different time and place before memories invade my mind, like one of those old video projectors with the reels and grainy pictures.

It is times like these I can remember my mother's voice perfectly. The images settle on one where I'm twirling around our living room in one of her frilly skirts pulled up to my armpits. The fabric of it, lifting in the air, twisting around me before I spin again and fall to my knees with the skirt circling around my small body.

"My beautiful, Shayla," my mother's voice would fall over me, brushing my skin and lighting my soul. "My perfect princess."

During these times, I remembered her beautiful heart-shaped face and long, straight black hair and green eyes the same shade as my own. She was beautiful... An angel with porcelain skin.

Then, the memory would shatter, and I was faced with the dark reality of my life with a drunk father who had died in a car accident and a stepmother, Belinda, who wanted me punished for being my mother's child– and punish me she did, coming up with new ways of torture at every turn.

Belinda stumbled into my room and the last pieces of my memories faded. She was clutching a bottle of wine in one hand and carrying the dress I was to wear that night in the other. It would be form-fitting... I knew that, but the pink color almost made me gag because it was meant to symbolize the innocence of a little girl, and I was far from innocent. I had lost that long ago.

She smiled, an evil glint sparking in her eyes. "You have a hair appointment, Princess," she gritted out, making the nickname my mother called me a dirty word.

I sat up, my heart in my throat, realizing she was almost gleeful as she told me. Belinda was never happy unless she was hurting me.

"Why?" My hair was the one thing I truly held onto because it reminded me of my mother. Would it be cut off? I wouldn't doubt that Belinda and Jim would serve up that punishment for me daring to try to leave them.

Belinda's brown eyes narrowed and she curled her lip as she slurred. "Just get ready."

Tears blurred my eyes as I pulled on my pants and t-shirt. A chill slid down the length of my neck, almost as if a gust of wind had decided to lick from my nape to shoulder.

I stepped out of the room as Belinda's hand gripped my biceps, digging her nails into the skin and moving the muscles painfully. She wrinkled her nose as if I was the disgusting one. One of Jim's bodyguards was there, a smirk on his face.

"We're not going to have any problems now, are we?" His eyes swept over my face, settling on my eyes as he licked his lips lasciviously. I suppressed a shudder. This particular goon enjoyed cruelty...Enjoyed my pain.

I shook my head, my heart hammering in my chest. "What is the stylist going to do to my hair?"

Belinda leaned into me, her alcohol-soaked breath caressing my ear, causing my body to tense as I gagged. "It's time to get rid of the goth look." I didn't understand how her voice was able to sound both bitchy and sugary at the same time. "After all, blondes have more fun."

My eyes widened and though I knew I shouldn't cause problems over something others saw as a minute thing...my hair, I couldn't help it. It was one of the few things I had of my mother since Belinda had thrown out everything I had that reminded me of her right after my father died. I shook my head as I jerked my arm out of Belinda's grasp and backed away.

"Mick, I think you might want to grab her. She looks like she's going to bolt," Belinda said, laughing as he lunged. I wasn't quick enough. He grasped me around my waist. His pelvis pressed against my bottom. I almost retched when I felt his erection against me. He was getting excited by my struggle.

I froze. All the fight left my body. To survive, I shouldn't struggle. To survive, I had to comply. As I was dragged out the door, I wondered how long it would be before doing things to survive would lose its importance because I no longer wanted to live.

I STOOD IN FRONT OF a group of men in the ghastly pink dress and the new blonde hair, shattered even more than what I had been before. Jim's hand was wrapped around my biceps in a way that would leave a bruise the next day, afraid I would bolt from the room even though I knew there was nowhere for me to run.

Men leered at me, reminding me of lions after a piece of meat is thrown in the middle of the cage, ready to fight each other for a taste. That's what this room was, the center of the cage I was locked in, even if there was no lock. I knew that even if I somehow escaped the room and stood in the town square, Jim would always have control over me, just as he controlled everything in town. No one would believe me.

"Smile at the gentlemen," he said, though not one of the men before me were gentlemen. Jim's voice was rough as he repeated the order to smile. I wondered what the town citizens would think if they ever heard this voice instead of the compelling voice he used while serving as their mayor. Every person in this room were predators. I glanced up at him as his fingers dug into my skin in a vice grip. Pain shot down my arm. It took everything in me not to cry out.

"You can force me to their beds, but you can't make me smile," I gritted out through clenched teeth.

"Do you remember what happens if you don't do as I say?" His voice was harsh against my ear.

Desi's tear-stained face invaded my mind and then the dead blue eyes of her brother, Hunter. My heart constricted as I realized that both of them had fallen because of me.

I forced a smile across my face as Jim's harsh glare settled on me, and he smirked because the bastard always got what he wanted. "Better."

He turned toward the men in the room. Many of those evil assholes had wives and children they would return to. He turned to them hungrily gazing at me. I could only hope they didn't prey on their own blood if they didn't win the lot to spend the night with me, but I could never be sure. My stomach churned.

"Gentlemen, your entertainment is pleased to be here," Sarcasm filled his voice as he released my arm and moved behind me. He stood straight and proud exuding his authority over everyone in the room. His fingers slid down the bare skin of my back as he slid down the zipper, opening it with slow movements. I stood as still as possible as every inch of my skin was laid bare for their gazes and the dress pooled at my heeled feet, reminding me of my mother's skirts I used to play dress up in.

I swallowed over the bile threatening to rise up my throat as I forced my gaze up because I didn't want any retaliation from Jim.

Shame flooded me as the men leered. Something drew my eyes toward the back of the room. My eyes landed on the young man who stood behind the letches, observing everything they were doing. My body chilled as recognition slid through my soul.

A tremble shuddered over me as I met a glare so angry I could feel the hate radiating from it.

"Hunter?" I whispered, catching Jim's attention.

As if Hunter realized I had seen him, his head tilted. His blue eyes still narrowed as the full force of his hate hit me in the chest.

He can't be here.
He's dead.

I closed my eyes, but when I opened them, he was still there. As if a cord had snapped on his self-control, he moved, dashing toward me as if to attack me. I was terrified of what he would do once he reached where I stood in front of the men. I threw my hands up, and I did the only thing my mind offered in protection... I screamed.

Chapter Three/Hunter

MY MOTHER ALWAYS PRAYED for the darkness not to reach us. She made us go to church, confess our sins, and hoped that we would be god-fearing children. Even before I died, I had moved far from her wishes. I was rebellious and, though I believed in something higher, I wasn't sure I believed in the god she prayed to.

Still, as I watched Shayla lying unconscious after the stress of seeing me took its toll on her, I wondered how my mother would feel about what I was doing now. There was a part of me, that after she fell unconscious felt that slice of guilt. The image of my mother lighting a candle drifted through my mind and for some reason that image had drained most of the energy I had accidentally obtained from the drunk man in the crowd who had walked through me. It stopped me from clasping Shayla's pretty neck in my grip.

I stared at my hands, realizing I was still reaching for her as her eyes opened and she turned her head, glancing around the room with wide eyes. Jim, who had been leaning against the wall, unaware that I was near, peered at her with a gaze that was almost wary and feigned care. I wondered if she knew he didn't really care for her... No one did.

"Hello, Princess," he said almost gently but she flinched when he spoke as her breaths heightened, moving quickly from between her trembling lips. "Can you tell me exactly what happened out there?"

A tremble slid down her spine, causing a ripple of fear to shake her whole body. "You didn't see him?" Her eyes were wide with fear as they took in the room around her searching for me.

"There were a lot of men in the crowd," he said, tilting his head as he peered at her. "You'll have to elaborate."

"Hunter..." My name died on her lips as Jim's eyes turned dark and dangerous and Shayla flinched.

"He's dead," he said, his voice turning cruel and twisted in a moment.

She shook her head, her newly dyed blonde hair hitting her in the face. "You're lying to me," she said, her lips trembling. "This is one of your sick games. I saw him alive. He was standing in the crowd staring at me."

Jim clenched his jaw and curled his fists. "If anyone is playing a game here, it's you, Shayla." his words hissed from between his lips, his body moving even closer. The dangerous aura around him darkened. "I assure you he's dead."

Tears slid down her cheeks. "But I—"

A crack sounded through the room as he backhanded her hard across the cheek. He leaned forward, an inch separating their faces. "Don't mention him again...He no longer exists."

She reached up to caress her cheek where the red impression of his hand remained. A sob broke from her lips and true terror settled into her expression.

"It's a game," she whispered, a tremor sliding through her. "It has to be."

Jim narrowed his eyes as he took off his suit jacket and advanced on her. "This is the only time I will say this," he said, sitting on the bed beside her. "He is dead...You saw his body. How can you doubt it?"

She closed her eyes and nodded as she took a deep breath before her body straightened. "You're right," she said, swallowing over her tears as her eyes took on a faraway expression. "I didn't see him. He's dead."

Acid boiled through my blood as he leaned forward and kissed her cheek where he had slapped her. "That's better, princess," he whispered against her skin. "Don't make me punish you anymore over this. He's dead. He's never coming back."

She nodded as his lips trailed to the tender spot of her neck and I realized with disgust that he was her lover as she continued to speak in an emotionless voice. "He's dead...He's never coming back."

"Because of you," I said, venom lacing through my voice as Jim covered her breast with one large hand.

She tensed at his touch. "Because of me," she choked out. I narrowed my eyes, and I wondered if she had heard me, two tears fell down her pale cheeks as she whispered again. "Because of me."

I reached forward and I touched her and for an instant I wondered if I was wrong, but the moment I did, I saw Desi's face. She was screaming and I realized I was able to view Shayla's memories when I touched her.

"Shayla, help me!" Her plea filled my ears as Jim held her down.

I backed away from Shayla, shattering the image, and narrowed my eyes as the wrath returned and the rest of my energy drained. She had been there. She had watched as my sister pleaded for her help. As my energy faded, I knew everything I did to her was well-deserved and she was going to pay... She was going to pay with her sanity and then, she was going to pay with her life. As I faded into the darkness so I could regain my energy, I envisioned those two tears sliding down her cheeks, determined to make more fall.

WHEN DARKNESS GAVE away to light, I found myself staring over Shayla's sleeping form. She was in her room now, the red mark on her cheek, quickly fading into a bruise. The spicy scent of Jim's cologne clung to her skin.

Anger enveloped me because she was sleeping peacefully after what she had done. I leaned forward, taking in each inch of her skin, wanting to mark it, leaving nothing recognizable behind. Before I harmed her body, though, I wanted to turn her mind into a kaleidoscope of pain. I wanted her sanity, turning her into a muddled mess. With the energy I had, I realized I could do that.

"Shayla," I whispered into her ear, causing her to jump. She scanned the room as she sat up. When her eyes settled on me, undisguised fear darkened her eyes as she took me in. She blinked, probably hoping I would disappear each time she opened her eyes.

She shook her head, her now blonde hair hitting her cheeks. "No," she whispered as a tremble slid over her bottom lip. She cringed away from me, her hands clutched the blanket as if searching for a sense of reality she could cling to. Too bad for her, she would never find that comfort again. "Y-You're dead. I-I saw you."

Tears squeezed from her eyes, falling down her cheek, leaving red marks behind as if they burned her skin. "And you must pay for that," I said, my voice holding a coldness I had never heard within it. It was dark, gritty and wrapped around the room like a snake. "And you will, because I will take everything from you for what you've done to me and Desi. You will lose your sanity...Your beauty...Everything you hold precious...and then? Then, I will take your life and you will die, Shayla. I will haunt you, taunt you, tear out your mind, and then, tear apart your body before you take that final breath. You deserve every bit of what I am going to do to you."

Her lips trembled. I bathed in her fear before I left the room. I needed to find more people to drain with a touch, as I had before to get the energy, I needed to enact my revenge. She screamed. It pierced the air with terror, pain and guilt, shattering any peace in its midst. A smile twisted across my face as dark satisfaction overtook me and my vengeance against Shayla Bell began.

Chapter Four/ Shayla

WHEN YOU LIVE A LIFE such as mine, you remember each kindness, each moment of joy, tucking them away in the only place those who wanted to hurt you can't touch. I had trained myself to relive those memories when the pain and torture became something too hard to face and threatened to break my mind. The memory would separate my mind from my body until I was able to face my life again.

The memory of my mother is often one of those precious, untouchable gems. It is truly the only memory that remains unsullied by anything that touches me now. However, there is another memory I've often held on to before it too became marred. It was an act of kindness on the same day that darkness destroyed what was left of my youth.

Even at the age of eleven, the beach was always a place where I would hide. My father's death brought a round of pain I was unable to process and the day the police officers arrived to deliver the news of his death; I ran toward the beach afraid of what life was going to be like for me under my stepmother's rule.

I sat beneath the pier, staring out at the waves. The ocean had always brought me peace. There was something about the way the waves crested and fell that soothed me and brought renewal. That day, it wasn't the waves that caught my attention.

On the beach, near the pier, was a boy of around my age building sandcastles. His black hair was wet on the ends, the water dripping down his tanned skin, mesmerizing me. When he glanced up, his eyes were the same breathtaking blue as the ocean I loved so much.

A little girl of about four ran up to him, laughing. Her dark pigtails bouncing as their mother and father laughed from the blanket beside them. My heart twisted with so much longing for a family such as theirs that I moved closer, wanting to feel just a piece of that perfection.

The boy's eyes moved toward me, sparkling when he saw me as a smile moved over his face. I involuntarily flinched, thinking he was going to be cruel.

"Do you want to help?" he asked, causing his mother to glance over in concern.

I froze for a moment as his mother's eyes darkened. She glanced around the shoreline before returning her gaze to me, tilting her head as she studied me. "Honey, where are your mother and father?"

I swallowed over the lump in my throat. My mother had been dead for years and my father had died the night before, but I didn't want to tell her that. I didn't want to ruin the perfect light of their family with my darkness. Instead, I glanced toward a little cabana near them that sold drinks to adults and pointed.

"My mother works over there." It was a lie, but I was already good at telling them because in my life, I had to learn to lie to avoid abuse. "She told me I can play as long as I stay out of the water."

The woman smiled, her face lighting up like my mother's once had, warming me soul deep. Then, nodded satisfied with the answer. After a few minutes, the little girl moved back to her parents as if afraid to stay away from them for too long. As the boy and I, tired of making the sandcastle, darted around the posts beneath the pier, laughing as we tried to catch each other.

When his hand closed around a bruise on my arm, I hissed and jerked back. His eyes darkened when they landed on the darkened spot. A frown crossed his brow.

"Did someone hurt you?" he asked as his eyes moved from the bruise to stare into my eyes.

I shook my head, but he stepped forward, his lips pursed as his eyes roamed over me, taking in each inch of my skin with concern. He stared at each bruise and each cut before those beautiful eyes moved back to my face. Tears burned my eyes. We had known each other for a matter of minutes, but I knew that our time together had ended. I was already grieving the end of my time of sun and laughter that he represented. I was grieving the end of my time with him.

"I-I have to leave," I said, shifting under his gaze. "I think my mom will be worried if I don't go back."

As I turned, he reached out and gripped my hand. "Wait!" he said, pulling me back toward him. "I won't ask you about it anymore but stay. I don't want you to go yet."

I studied him as fractured emotions sliced through me, confusing me, and making me leery of his reasons for wanting me to stay.

"Why are you being nice to me?" I asked, the suspicion that people were basically mean sliding through me.

He frowned. "Aren't people usually nice to you?"

I shook my head, surprising myself with my honesty. "No."

He tilted his head, confusion wrapping around him. "I don't understand why." He shifted as his cheeks colored, turning his tanned skin pink. "You're nice, and pretty."

I shrugged. For some reason, his compliment made me want to cry more. "It doesn't matter to them."

He surprised me when he wrapped his arms around me. A tear fell down my cheek. When he backed away, his gaze caught on the tear traveling with it until he reached forward and captured it on the tip of his finger.

"Don't cry," he whispered, before pressing his lips against mine.

The kiss was perfect in its innocence. I inhaled sharply as he pulled away. "Why did you do that?"

"It's what my dad does when my mom cries," he said, shifting as his cheeks turned from pink to scarlet. "He says it makes her happy again. I wanted you to feel better."

I smiled as my body warmed, threading those fractured feelings of confusion and suspicion into something much brighter. I had never kissed a boy, nor had one kissed me. The sweetness of his gesture healed something in me... At least in that moment.

"Thank you," I said, blushing further when I realized I didn't know his name. I realized I wanted to know it badly so I could take it with me. Then, I would have it to recall when it seemed no one else cared for me– to remember this boy did, even if it was only for a few minutes. Still, I was afraid and ashamed to give him my real name. I didn't want this beautiful family marred by my life of pain. Instead, I gave him the name of my mother.

"My name is Ellie," I whispered, shifting the sand beneath my feet. "If we're going to be friends, I think you should have a name to call me by."

His lips twitched into a grin, lighting up his face. "My name is Hunter... Hunter De Haven."

In that moment when Hunter raged out of the room the memory crashed around me as a new ache settled into my heart. The memory I had used to save me from some of my darkest hours was a bitter irony. I had helped destroy the one family who I had admired...The one family who had given me peace. The boy who had given me my first kiss so I wouldn't cry would become the cause of more tears because I had been the reason for his death. The love I had always carried for him would be returned with blinding hate because of selfishness on my part. There would be no protection from it, because how could I protect myself when I could no longer remember his kindness without realizing that his family's downfall was my fault? How could I fight against his revenge when I deserved every single act of torture he would give me?

Chapter Five/ Hunter

I NEVER THOUGHT ABOUT how much energy people, objects and things contained until my death nor how the energy flowed between them. It exchanged constantly, leaving one person energized and another drained. Those who were ill or injured I stayed away from, terrified I would kill an innocent. Those who were drunk or high gave very little energy, which explained why the energy I received from the drunk man dwindled so quickly.

As I walked through the town, pulling energy from those unfortunate enough to come in contact with me, I realized those who held power over others possessed more than the ones who were powerless. So, I focused on those who took advantage of others until I rested against a light pole and drained the energy from it until the bulb exploded above me in a shower of sparks and glass. It caused the surrounding people to stare at it with large wary eyes. I pulsed with bright light until it absorbed into my being. This time, the energy I absorbed would not fade so quickly, and Shayla would have to face me for as long as it remained.

I touched another light pole and another until I was able to control every aspect of myself, testing my visibility out on a drug dealer. I faded in front of him, causing him to piss his pants before making my way back to Shayla's town home in the richer part of town.

I curled my lip in disgust as I entered her home, finding her stepmother on the couch, an empty bottle beside her and another half empty bottle on the table in front of her. I was happy she wouldn't run to Shayla's rescue when she started crying... And I would make her cry and scream until her voice faded.

When I reached her room, I found her on her bed with her eyes closed and started getting mad. How could she be sleeping peacefully again? Then I noticed the way her chest rose and fell. She wasn't sleeping yet. I studied her. Her face was beautiful. I wouldn't deny that, but it was a mask covering every ugly aspect of her true self to everyone else in the world but me.

She was evil. She introduced Desi's abuser to her. I wondered if there were more girls that she lured to Jim... If there was more death that could be laid at her feet. As I stared at her, I wondered what other crimes she committed. The answer would probably be dark and gritty, making her outer beauty fade to me even more.

"Wake up, princess," I said, my lips curling in disgust around the name Jim had called her. I would ruin that precious nickname, too. She wouldn't have anything she could hold dear. She flinched, opening her eyes to peer into mine. Her expression reflected the fear that I would feed until it became so big it consumed her.

She saw me. She rushed back against the wall at the head of her bed, as far as she could get from me. She curled in a tight ball and closed her eyes, as if she could block out my image. She shook so much the bed trembled. Any bravery she had gained in my absence fled as tears fell down her cheeks leaving red marks in their wake.

"You're dead," she whispered, rocking back and forth, her lips trembling over the words before repeating them in a wavering voice.

"Because of you," I gritted out, stepping closer to her bed, the fury and hate sliding from me into her. "Because of you, I'm dead, and Desi's life has been tainted. Because of you, my family is in tatters. How many more families have you destroyed? How many more people have you destroyed or gotten killed?"

Her trembling visibly increased. Her eyelids pressed together, whispering to herself that I wasn't real... I wasn't really in her presence but as if she knew there was no possibility of that, her eyes burst open and beautiful despair washed over her face so potent that it shook through me giving my vengeance more life.

"I hope you enjoyed your sleep while I was gone," I said, giving her a cruel smile. "Because you will not get a moment of rest in my presence. You will only feel misery and pain."

She blinked as another tear fell down her cheek, accepting her fate. Her complacency wasn't enough to feed me. Her tears alone would never be enough. I stepped forward as her eyes followed my every move, widening as I tilted my head. She stiffened, waiting for my attack.

"You think you're strong," I said, gritting my teeth as my rage pulsed through me. I wanted her screams, not her silent acceptance. I wanted her to fight, so she knew exactly what I was taking from her. I wanted her will to live to fade slowly, not drain in one moment. "But you're nothing but a dirty, murdering slut. You're weak, and I will show you exactly how weak you truly are."

My anger drove me. I reached forward as power pulsed through me, gripping her neck as I pulled her from the bed easily, slamming her against the wall hard enough to cause it to shake. She inhaled sharply as her eyes met mine. Images of the beach flashed in front of my eyes, trapping my consciousness in a day that had been forever ingrained upon my memory... Ellie... That kiss... My first kiss.

Shock and rage like no other slammed through me as I realized why recognition always niggled at my mind, telling me I knew her. She lied to me and my family from the beginning and I had given a piece of myself to her that day... No, not her... The girl I believed her to be... Ellie, the nervous, beautiful girl. The girl I always searched for in every face since that moment... The girl I gave my first kiss to because of a connection I had always stupidly believed bound us. She lied and manipulated me from the beginning. She destroyed my family when they had shown her nothing but kindness. She befriended my sister only to darken her life... her soul... And then, she had taken that memory... That image of a girl I had held onto every day since I met her and ruined it... Taking something else precious to me when I assumed she had already taken everything.

I was stupid... So stupid because I always believed she held onto that memory like the precious, untouchable moment I always assumed it was. All the ridiculous fantasies of meeting her again crashed around me like nails on a slate floor.

The fury and hurt were all-consuming. My hand slammed through her chest, gripping her heart, savoring its beats within the palm of my hand as I gripped it, restricting its movement. "How could you do this to us?"

Her eyes widened as she gasped for breath but didn't fight against it. It was as if she was welcoming death, and that alone kept me from taking her life. I would never give her anything she wanted. Each breath she took would be filled with torture, in payment for all the pain she had caused.

"You're not dying yet, Shayla," I hissed in her face, releasing her heart, but kept my hand around her throat. "You won't die until I allow it. You will beg for it, and I will still deny you. I will break down every defense you have and destroy you for every single thing you've taken from me and those I love. You'll live every second with the fear that I am right behind you, beside you, or in front of you."

Tears slid from her chin, sliding through my hand at her throat and I could sense her emotions within them... Guilt... Anger... Remorse... Grief...Acceptance... Love. Most made sense to me, but the last one didn't. I released her, allowing her to fall to the floor. She curled into a ball as her body trembled. My nostrils flared as I realized the only love she felt was toward herself, and I was determined to turn every ounce of it into hate.

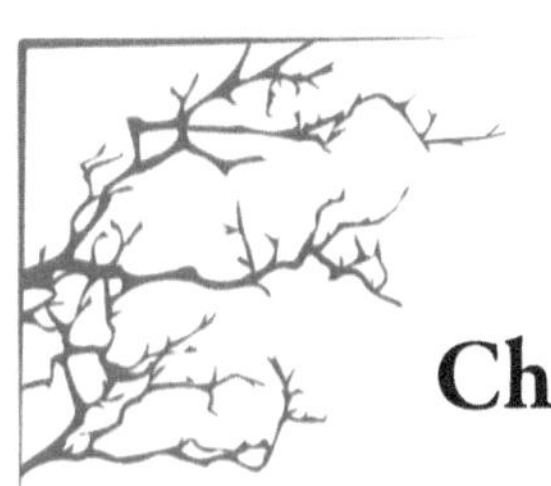

Chapter Six/ Shayla

SHAME... IT WAS A CONSTANT emotion that spread through my soul, rotting me from the inside out, taking little pieces of the girl I had once been, when my mother was alive. I always experienced it when my dad was so drunk he didn't realize or care when Belinda called me stupid or pushed me or hit me. He didn't fight against her when she lied and accused me of things I never did, and he got his razor strap out and beat me until I fell to the ground sobbing, my skin bleeding and bruised... Until I no longer felt the pain with the first few slaps. That's when Belinda started wetting the strap before those beatings, making sure I felt each blow against my skin.

I learned not to speak or show emotion that would cause me to cry. If I did, Belinda would use those tears and twist it into a punishment that became even worse. I learned how to lie to save myself from punishment and embarrassment and be suspicious of everyone because if I let down walls... If I let them in; they were likely to hurt me.

Belinda was always someone to regard with suspicion. She would make sure each word I uttered could be used. I couldn't sleep without worrying that she would cut my hair or worse and I knew better than to eat anything she cooked. There was no moment of kindness. I always... always got sick. The insults added to my shame. I was stupid... A slut like my mother... Too fat... Worthless... So worthless. Then my dad died and what little protection he gave me disappeared.

The day I met Hunter at the beach, Belinda had called the police and reported me as a runaway. That's when I met Jim. The police officer had been one of his cronies. My shame only deepened. Money exchanged hands between Jim and Belinda. Then, on my twelfth birthday, he took the one precious proof of my innocence. He called it a birthday present.

After that fateful night, I would be pulled from my room, dressed pretty and betted on by men just like Jim... Men who wanted to take their piece of flesh... Mar me even further and possess more than my body because their images remained engraved in my mind to haunt my nightmares. Sometimes, they would even haunt my days, if I happened upon one of them pretending... Always pretending to be the perfect family men or men who helped the community but I understood who they were... The true dredges of society.

When one of them turned out to be a teacher at my school, I realized escaping would be impossible. Jim had eyes everywhere.

So, I didn't try to fight. As long as I didn't fight, my days away from him were mine to do what I pleased. So, I volunteered at the community center, hoping to balance the good with the bad. That's where I found Desi.

I wasn't sure, when I first saw her, if she was the same little girl I had seen at the beach. It was only when Hunter picked her up that I knew. The shame made me hide from him every time he arrived. The fear he would look into me and view those ugly dark spots that Jim left behind made me stay away and, of course, there was the lie I had told him... My name.

So, I stayed close to Desi... That piece of him, the boy I would always love. As I grew closer to her, I realized that I loved her like a sister. She became my only friend. Desi and Hunter made me want to escape. As my eighteenth birthday drew close, I realized I would be able to. I would escape the town to a place where Jim didn't hold power.

The day before my birthday, Jim called me to his home. One more day... I remember thinking one more day... One more time before I left somewhere safe. However, when I stepped into his house, that hope faded. I realized the mistake I had made.

He was holding Desi down. Tears flowed down her cheeks as he touched her... Intimately. I noticed with relief he hadn't raped her yet but touching her was bad enough. Desperation took flight in my chest beckoning me to sacrifice myself into the darkness for her sake. Desi could not become me. It tore my soul in two, and I shuddered as my eyes met hers.

"Shayla, help me," she pleaded, reaching for me. My stomach twisted and a protectiveness I had never experienced for anyone else slammed through me. It caused me to fight against a man I had learned never to even speak against.

"Leave her alone," I whimpered, stepping forward, but Jim's bodyguards stepped from the shadows to hold me back.

"You're going to leave me," Jim said, through his teeth. "I won't stop you, Shayla, but when you do, she will take your place and what has happened so far will become much worse. She will lose that little innocent piece of her, the same innocent piece you held so precious, and it will be all your fault."

My lip quivered as my dreams of escape crashed down around me. My eyes met hers and I would have given anything to go back to the day I saw her again and run in the opposite direction to protect her... To protect her from me. My love for anyone was toxic and now it had hurt her. The only thing I could do was keep her from getting hurt worse.

"Let her go," I said, the tears scalding my cheeks and dripping into my soul.

"Say you're mine for life and I will," he said, narrowing those terrifying eyes of his on me.

I understood from that moment on, he would have my every move watched to prevent my escape. I would remain trapped for life, but it was better than sentencing Desi to that same fate.

I swallowed back the bile that had churned from my stomach, understanding exactly why Jim was doing this. It wasn't sex he wanted. Power is what got him off and I would give him that power if he would leave Desi alone. "I'm yours... f-for life," I stumbled over the words damning my life as surely as I damned my soul. "Let her go."

He released her, and I stepped forward, straightening her dress before pulling her toward me, trying to calm her from something that had darkened her. Her sobs soaked into me becoming a part of me that would haunt my worst nightmares.

"Go home," I whispered, kissing the top of her head. I realized later I should have told her not to tell... It would put those she loved in danger. Another mistake of mine.

She raised her head, and I recognized that same darkness I carried in my soul in hers. He had marked her, but maybe... Maybe she would be alright if she escaped. Maybe she would have a life.

"Sh-Shayla," she said in a voice so small I barely heard her. "He's gonna hurt you."

I cupped her cheeks in my hands, that shame sliding through me again as the despair of the situation washed over me. "I'm used to it. I can handle it. You don't need to," I cried, shaking. "I love you, Desi. Go home and forget I ever existed."

The bodyguards pulled her away from me and I faced Jim as he rolled up his shirt sleeves. I waited for the first blow, because no matter what he did to me, it would never be as bad as what he had done to Desi.

I understood in a moment that her downfall was my fault. When they pulled me into the room the next night to view Hunter's dead body, I understood whose hands were red with his blood. As Hunter almost killed me and promised torture... I knew I deserved every bit of it. Because I loved Desi... Jim had hurt her and because Hunter loved his sister, Jim had killed him. Still, my love had started it all. My love was poisonous... Toxic enough to kill. I deserved every single blow Hunter would give me. I deserved to die.

Chapter Seven/Hunter

A FLICKERING FLAME danced in front of my eyes as the image of my mother lighting a candle whispered in my brain. I shoved my hands against my eyes, trying to make it stop, not understanding why this image came to me during my worst acts of wrath against Shayla. Still, it remained, fading into another of my mother praying, her rosary beads moving through her pale hands as words I did not understand flowed over her lips. Her eyes closed, but the strain there was evident.

I stared at Shayla, seeing the girl I had thought she was that day at the beach for an instant as she laid where she fell at my feet. Her breaths came in labored pants as her hand curled around the spot where my hand had entered her chest. Sweat fell from her brow. I struggled to hold on to the wrath as the face of the young girl she had once been melted into the girl she was now.

"Get up," I said, but my voice didn't hold the anger from before.

Still, she didn't move. I narrowed my eyes as the annoyance returned. "I said get up!" I shouted, but she only flinched, remaining on the floor, her sobs becoming louder.

"Look at me," I said, my voice low as the anger began to come back. My mother's image praying for me was replaced with the image of Desi's tears. "Look at what you've caused. Look at the one whose life you took."

She stiffened as she raised her head. Her pale skin was blotched with tears. She flinched again as her eyes touched mine. Fear and guilt twisted her tear-streaked face, but it wasn't enough to assuage the pain and harm she had done to my family. I wanted her to confess her sins. I wanted her to admit them.

"Tell me why you did this," I said, through gritted teeth, but still she said nothing. She didn't admit it, nor did she defend herself, and it pissed me off even more. I wanted her to speak. I wanted an explanation for my family's demise under her hand. I wanted her to say something to help me hang onto the anger and the wrath that could fade with a simple image of my mother with her head bowed.

She stared at me. Her tears fell down her face in broken paths, leaving red streaks as if they burned her. Her lips twitched as if she wanted to say something, but instead, another sob broke from her. My hands fisted at my side as my rage boiled over and any pity I had experienced for her vanished along with that guilt that prevented me from acting on further torture.

"You're a liar and a murderer," I growled, bending toward her, causing her to flinch. "You manipulated us... You manipulated Desi."

Another whimper broke from her at the mention of my sister's name, only fueling me more as she shook her head. "Your tears mean nothing. Her tears mean everything. You broke her."

"I know," she whispered, but those two words did nothing to quell the immense flame of anger slicing through my soul.

"I wish she never met you!" I screamed, causing her to flinch. "I wish I had never met you!"

Her bottom lip trembled as her eyes met mine, despair coloring her features as she whispered. "I wish for that too."

I narrowed my eyes, my body pulsing with rage. Of course, she wished she hadn't met us because now it was going to result in her torture and death.

"Get up!" I screamed, wanting her to stand and face me. Still, she stayed curled on the floor, staring at me with eyes that reminded me of a girl I thought was kind and pure and perfect.

I reached for her, wrapping my hand around her neck, my fingers pressed into her skin. Images of Desi crying out for her hit me, causing me to tighten my hold around her neck. Her first tear hit me, sliding through my skin. Her fear washed over me, but it wasn't fear of me. It was fear of the man I thought was her lover. It was fear of Jim. The image of Desi shifted, and I saw the day he took her innocence. The sick bastard said it was her birthday present. Another memory of Shayla's wormed through my vision when he displayed her, and bets were placed to be with her by the dredges of the town.

Another tear hit me, and I felt her remorse and shame as she was called names and beaten by her stepmother, dad, Jim and some of the men who won her. Then, the moment she told me her name was Ellie and the shame that came from it because she didn't want me to know what type of life she lived. I trembled as my hand loosened but didn't move from her neck. Her pulse hammered against my fingertips.

The next tear brought grief so immense that my soul bled with it, slicing through it like razors sliding against my heart as her mother's image slid through my mind.

Then, another dropped through my soul, swamping me with love so immense but so torturous that it caused a sob to break from me. Love for her mother. Love for me that lived beyond that summer day and helped her through her darkest hours... Love for Desi as she sacrificed herself and trapped herself in a town with monsters that preyed on her everywhere. Love that made her take the beating that came after Desi left without fighting back.

My eyes met hers and I felt the final tear as acceptance washed over me, but it was acceptance of guilt that was not hers to bear... Guilt I had placed on her and the willingness to die for it.

I took a deep breath and staggered away from her, all the energy I had gained fading quickly.

A tear fell from my eye as all the rage was replaced with my own guilt, my own remorse as I realized she had always been the same girl I loved every day since meeting her and I had done nothing but torture her for loving me back.

My body flickered as I whispered, my voice choked with the mistake I had made... Words that would never be enough. "I'm sorry."

I floated in nothingness as my soul was sliced in two by everything I had said and done to Shayla... An innocent in everything. She had been tortured by what had happened to Desi... To me. All she had received in return for her love, care and sacrifice was hate and vengeance. Shayla had become my victim just as she was a victim to everyone else in her life. I had taken a safe memory that helped her get through her darkness and made it something that held guilt and I should never be forgiven for that. I would never forgive myself.

I stayed in that nothingness for an immeasurable amount of time, my mind becoming my own torture and punishment for harming Shayla further. I wondered if this was where I would stay, facing my own personal hell... One I had created.

Then I began to fade to that place of darkness with the voice of the being who had given me a chance at justice, whispering through my mind. "Remember, the path to things that may be justified is dark and twisted. It is a journey of many forks and turns. Be sure what you choose to do, so it doesn't darken your soul."

As darkness completely took me, I realized Shayla was the path to my justice, but she wasn't the one who deserved my vengeance. Those who had hurt her were. It didn't just end with her stepmother or Jim. Every single person who touched her deserved to have justice meted out for them for their crimes and that justice would no longer only be for me or Desi but for Shayla, too. I had taken a wrong turn, but it led me to this point. Shayla was no longer my target. She was someone I was going to protect. She was someone I was going to free.

Chapter Eight/Shayla

SILENCE CRASHED AROUND me and all that was left was the remnants of the apology Hunter left behind gathering in my mind like shadows. His words echoed through my soul cutting me more thoroughly than his actions taking chunks of my already fractured sanity and twisting the pieces in confusion and shame because I didn't understand. Why did he apologize when I deserved every single act he had committed against me? I deserved death. I had earned it all.

An immeasurable amount of time ticked by before I pulled myself up to stand on wobbly legs with the support of the wall and shuffled across the room. My weary body ached all over, but especially my throat where the apparition, where Hunter, had choked me. I collapsed on the bed, trembling as regret washed through me, prickling my skin before sinking into me. For the millionth time, I wished I had been strong enough to have saved Desi... And Hunter. I wish I had been strong enough to save myself. My weakness was my downfall. Guilt took possession of my soul.

The memory of Hunter's face twisted in anger was the worst type of torture...His eyes, darkened by pain, was a punishment even the bowels of hell couldn't match. His hands squeezing my throat brought every reason I should die to the surface.

It was lunacy how I felt about him in those moments. I didn't hate him. Instead, the real torture was that I still loved him even as he sought to bring my death and I knew, even after I perished, I would still hold him dear even as I burned in the pits of hell.

I closed my eyes, so tired of feeling... So tired of hurting... So tired of living. I was damaged... I was broken... Unfixable... Unlovable. The evidence of my cowardice was plain. I was weak... So weak.

I'd long since given up on sleep. I sat, rocking on my bed, these thoughts tumbling through my head on an endless cycle for hours. The doorknob to my room jiggled and I scooted under the covers before the door opened, pretending I was asleep. I didn't move. Whoever was there was just another means of torture, and I wasn't going to help them administer it. I was tired of helping them bring about my pain.

Breaths in the darkness and the scent of alcohol moved over me with the same impact as a razor against the skin. I stiffened, realizing this wasn't Belinda or Jim. This was one of the men with no name who had bet on me. I had been paid for and was expected to deliver. I was so tired of delivering.

He said my name, his breaths rushing from him with excitement. When I didn't respond, he gripped my hair, jerking me out of bed and towards him. Tears sprang to my eyes as strands of hair were ripped from the roots. "Don't pretend to be asleep, whore," his voice was slurred and poisoned with the warning of caution... Telling me not to fight... Not to resist.

I swallowed hard, recognizing the voice of one of the aristocrats in the town...A man who came from old money...A man people were afraid to go against because he was able to do whatever he wanted with no consequences.

He pulled me to face him. His slap against my face was expected but still, I cried with the force of it as my bottom lip split down the center. The metallic taste of blood entered my mouth as he backhanded me again, causing me to fall. Blood dripped from my nose mixing with tears as they fell from my eyes.

"On your knees," he demanded, and I knew that to deny him would make my beating worse. Still, I would face anything not to be forced to do the sinful things swirling in his evil mind.

"No," my voice was weak, but I was proud I had said it.

He curled his fists, his lips twisting in rage. "You don't get to deny me. You're bought and paid for," he growled. "On your goddamn knees."

He came toward me as I scrambled to my feet. I don't know where I got the strength or the bravery, but I pushed him away, taking him by surprise and causing him to stumble and fall. My hands curled at my sides.

"I said no!" I screamed, the rush of emotions stronger than the fear.

He stood; his blue eyes narrowed as he sobered. Moonlight from the window bounced off his bald head as he cracked his knuckles. He came toward me again, his face red.

I tried to dart past him, but he jerked me backwards by the hair, more forceful than before, slamming me to the ground so hard my breath was knocked from me. He straddled my waist, his angry face hovering over me as his hand curled around my neck, squeezing until black dots danced in front of my eyes.

His fist curled as he punched me in the stomach. Pain exploded through my abdomen as I gasped for breath. Still, I tried to fight him as he ripped the lace night shirt I was wearing down the middle baring my breasts to him. His mouth descended upon me, his teeth bruising my skin as I fought weakly against him. Tears heated my face. He had me. There was no escape.

A roar echoed through the room but the man above me didn't react. I blinked away the tears that were blurring my vision. Hunter was standing above us, his face twisted in a rage so potent that it pushed away the shame of him witnessing me like this. He reached forward, his hand entering my attacker's chest, causing him to stiffen. His eyes widened in surprise.

"He won't touch you again," His teeth were bared as I blinked. His words didn't make sense because he *wanted* my pain. He *wanted* me to die.

The man above me began to gasp, releasing me to clutch at his chest. A strangled sound burst from his throat before he fell on top of me. I screamed. His body spasmed, crushing me beneath him. I couldn't breathe and started to panic. A long exhale escaped his throat, and then, his breaths ceased. I stared at Hunter as he pushed the man away from me with a booted foot.

A white light moved out of the man, floating above his body before gliding into Hunter. He flickered for a moment before becoming more vivid than before. I realized he had absorbed the man's spirit.

My eyes widened as I stared at the man's body. His eyes were open, but they were lifeless. His chest didn't rise or fall.

"You killed him," I whispered, but I didn't feel remorse. Instead, I experienced relief because he wouldn't touch me anymore...He wouldn't touch anyone else. The damage he had done to me and countless other girls ended with his last breath.

I blinked, turning my head to gaze up at Hunter. His expression was still tense. Anger radiated through his spectral form. I trembled as so many questions fired through my mind. I had no answers because only a few hours before, Hunter had wanted my death. For a moment, I wondered if he somehow changed his mind...If he somehow wanted to save me. Maybe he didn't want to see the light fade from my eyes.

Maybe he wants to be the one to do it, my thoughts offered. *Maybe that's why he saved you.*

It was the only thing that made sense. Panic seized me as he reached for me because, though I wanted death, I still feared the pain that would come with it. Hunter wanted my pain. He wanted to drive me insane before killing me. He had admitted that. As the images of what he could do to me played through my head, I gave into the fear and became the coward I was and opened my mouth and screamed.

Chapter Nine/ Hunter

IT WAS TOO LATE...IT echoed through my mind breaking through my soul like shattered glass. Her screams pierced me, and I knew her insanity at that moment was the fault of everyone who had hurt her, and I was one of those people.

I faded enough, taking away my image but still, she screamed, slicing pieces of my already broken soul, drenching them in her pain and sorrow and I knew... I knew I had to save her even if it meant losing myself in her darkness... Losing myself in mine.

"Shayla, I won't hurt you," I whispered, my voice as broken as the rest of me. My soul trembled with a new energy, swamping through me begging me to protect her. "I know none of this was your fault."

Her screams halted as she pulled her knees to her chest and sobbed, whispering something over and over as she rocked back and forth, rhythmically moving with the tempo of each word. I moved close enough to hear.

"It is. It is. It is," she was repeating, terrifying me further that she could think that, but then, I could not remember one time she had denied it, nor could I remember when she had fought back.

"No, Shayla," I whispered, wanting to touch her but I knew she would no longer be on the edge of insanity but drowning in the depths of it if I did.

"Please just end it," she begged, her plea burning me like acid. "Please just k-kill me. I-I deserve it."

I shook my head though she couldn't see it, refusing to take something as precious as her life.

"I won't," I said, horrified that she truly wanted her life to end. The guilt that I had pushed her to that point ran through me like a dagger to my heart.

She raised her head and the darkness in her eyes caused me to flinch away from her. Anguish poured out of her body.. Her past and her present offered no hope for happiness or peace. Her lip trembled as blood trickled down her chin from her split lip dripping in scarlet streams on the pale skin of her chest.

"I promise I will make this right," I said, and she flinched, more tears falling down her cheeks. My soul wrenched because she was so afraid of me. "I'm going to punish everyone who ever hurt you."

The door opened and her stepmother stumbled inside. She stopped as she glanced from Shayla to the man lying motionless on the floor. She moved further into the room tilting her head as her gaze remained on the man's corpse. A chill slid down my spine as I realized how calm she seemed about the man's death.

"What did you do, you whore?" She spat and then shook her head, "Jim is going to be furious with you."

Shayla closed her eyes, releasing more tears. Her stepmother saw the blood and torn clothes, her eyes narrowing further. There was no concern for Shayla's safety. There was no love there at all.

"At least he got his pound of flesh before you killed him," she said, rolling her eyes and then, pulled a cell phone from her pocket. "You deserve it for all the problems you just caused."

"I didn't kill him," Shayla whispered but her stepmother didn't listen. Instead, she pushed buttons on the cellphone.

"Jim, we've got a problem here," she said, her foot tapping on the ground in a rhythm that drove me crazy. Shayla's eyes opened and focused on it, flinching each time the tips of the woman's toes fell upon the ground, making me wonder if she did this each time she tried to hurt Shayla.

Shayla hugged her knees tighter becoming a shadow of herself. That sweet girl that I met at the beach so long ago fled further into the recesses of my mind only to be replaced by this girl who brought a deep sense of sadness to me, and yet, I loved her so much more.

I reached forward, hoping I could figure out what to do, almost jerking back but realizing it was the only way I had to help her. With a barely-there brush of my fingertips, I touched a tear. She was so lost that she didn't even notice that I touched her. The tear brought grief so great that I shuddered with it as a memory stuttered to life.

Her stepmother stood in a dirty kitchen taking money from Jim, an evil smirk on her face. "As long as you continue to pay me, you can do whatever you want to the little bitch," she whispered, glancing at a young Shayla sitting on the couch in a decrepit apartment. I realized with horror that she was wearing the same clothes she had worn on the day I met her. I jerked my hand away understanding her stepmother had sold her that same day.

Anger took over as I glanced at Shayla and then, the evil woman who should have cared for her but instead, hurt her in the most heinous way possible. She may not have raped her, but she was just as guilty in it as Jim was. It was obvious she knew exactly what he was going to do. More importantly, she had started it all, taking away the only innocence Shayla had left. Now, I knew where I would begin my revenge. I would do everything I promised to do to Shayla to the woman who started it all with her cold heart full of greed.

She stepped toward Shayla as if intending to hit her. I glanced at her still curled on the floor, realizing she was too fragile to see me.

Instead, I moved forward and pushed the woman away causing her to stumble and fall to the shiny, wooden planks beneath her feet. A flicker of her memories slid into my mind, and I realized in that instant, her crimes were much worse than I originally thought.

She was younger in the vision; her face lacked the wrinkles years of drinking had given her, but cruelty still twisted her face. She was talking to a man, handing him money.

"Are you sure you wanna do this?" The man asked, scratching his beard.

"Of course, I do," she said, grinning crookedly. "You know I've always wanted what I want, and Nick won't date me while she's still alive. He's still so hung up on her, he won't even notice me."

"What's her name and how do you want it done?" The guy asked, frowning.

"Her name is Ellie...Ellie Bell," Belinda said, raising her chin, her hatred seeping through her pores. "And I don't care how you do it as long as she's gone for good."

She handed him a picture of a woman who looked remarkably like Shayla had with dark hair. The man nodded his head.

"Alright, Belinda," he said, grinning, his sickening, wicked intentions clear. "I think I know exactly what I'm going to do with her."

"Just don't get caught," she said with a shrug. It disturbed me that Belinda was so nonchalant about a woman's death. "That would be bad for both of us."

"Don't worry," he smirked as he took out a knife. "I've done this many times before."

The memory faded, and I narrowed my eyes at the woman who had caused Shayla so much pain, as she glanced around trying to figure out what had caused her to stumble and fall.

I leaned toward her and whispered into her ear, "Murderer."

She glanced around the room, frowning. "What the hell?" She shook her head, her back straight, glancing around again. She sighed, rolling her eyes. "Now, I'm starting to hear things."

I raised my brow. I refused to have her believe that she was imagining things... Imagining me. I wanted her sanity. I wanted it all.

I leaned toward her again. "Murderer."

She jerked away from me; her hand flying to her chest as she glanced around the room. When she couldn't find anything to explain what she was hearing, her eyes filled with fear as she began to question everything around her. Her bottom lip trembled. I gritted my teeth, stopping myself from doing anything further because I wanted this woman's torture to be slow. I wanted her to question everything around her before I showed myself. I wanted her to feel every bit of pain she had given to Shayla before I caused her to take her final breath.

Chapter Ten/ Shayla

MURDERER... THE WORD pierced my brain, scattering into fragments, making it hard to focus on anything else. Moments before the word had been uttered, she had acted as if she were going to hit me, but before her fist was able to connect with my flesh, she had stumbled upon the floor almost as if someone had pushed her. I wondered if Hunter kept her from striking me. If he did, it meant he spoke the truth when he said he was going to protect me. The thought twisted my mind in confusion even more because I didn't deserve any kindness from him. Not after everything I had done.

When he spoke, I thought Hunter had spoken to me, but it soon became clear he didn't. The word had been directed toward Belinda.

I raised my brow at her. She was glancing around the room with wild brown eyes. Her face was pale, only becoming paler at the mention of that word... Murderer.

I frowned because, though Belinda was many things, she had never killed anyone. A tremble slid down her spine and I realized in all the years I knew her, I had never once seen her afraid, but it was obvious she was frightened now. I stared at her as warmth moved through me. It was satisfying to realize that she could experience the emotion she had elicited in me every day since my father introduced me to her. It was vindicating that she could tremble as she worried about someone striking her.

"Did you hear that?" She asked, glancing around again. Her hand fluttered to her throat. "Do you have someone in here?"

I licked my lips, hissing at the pain slicing through the cut, and gazed into her eyes before shaking my head. She glanced around the room again, finding no place to hide anyone before turning back to me. Her bottom lip trembled. Her fear there made her more human. I wanted to have her experience the emotion as long as possible. Perhaps I should have felt guilty over it, but I didn't. Instead, my whole soul churned with a sense of Justice. It was something I rarely witnessed happening when it came to my life.

"No, I didn't hear anything and there is no one else here, to my knowledge," I lied, but it was amongst the thousands of lies I had told over my lifetime to keep her from administering pain. It was ironic that this time I lied to cause her pain.

She opened her mouth, but nothing came out as her fear took her voice. The door opened and Jim entered, his bodyguards flanking his sides, almost stepping on Belinda as they entered. He glanced at my face and the ripped nightshirt before his eyes settled on the man on the floor, taking in his form with an air of apathy before shrugging. He barely looked at Belinda.

"What happened, Shayla?" He asked, his voice deceptively smooth. I understood, like many times before, that how I answered determined whether I was punished or not. I swallowed over the lump in my throat. Jim took a step closer to me. I realized the danger of not formulating an answer before he reached me and forced words from between my lips.

"He was being rough with me," I whispered, my voice small, deciding to stick to the truth as much as possible. I twisted the bottom of my tattered nightgown in my hands. Blood dripped down my face on the back of my hand. I stared at the stark crimson against the paleness of my skin as I continued. "His face turned red, he gripped his chest, and he fell on me. Then I noticed he wasn't breathing anymore."

Jim went to the man, inspecting the man as he turned him over with the toe of his boot. "There are no bruises," he said, inspecting the body. "I'm sure the old boy had a heart attack. It's a good thing he paid before he came here. Otherwise, I would be much more upset."

Jim moved toward me, gripping my chin, I hissed as he reopened the cut on my lip with the motion. More blood dripped down my chin. I wanted to recoil from him as his brown eyes narrowed, studying my face. His eyes swept over me in disgust as he saw the damage the man had done to my face.

"It serves him right," he said, shaking his head before backing away from me. "They aren't supposed to bruise your face. No one will bid on you like this. I'll be out of a lot of money."

Bile churned in my stomach, causing the taste to fill my mouth at the thought of being forced to be with another one of those men, but I knew better than to protest. That would only gain another punishment from Jim.

He stood and turned to his men, curling his lip as he jerked his head toward the body. "Get him out of here," he ordered, and they immediately did his bidding, picking the man's body up from the floor and pulling him out the door.

Jim shook his head. "It's a shame," he said with a sigh. "He brought in a lot of money. I need to find more bidders."

His eyes fell on Belinda, his mouth pressed into a thin line. He raised a brow. "Why are you on the floor?"

Belinda's eyes were still darkened in fear as they rose to meet his. "I-I guess I drank too much," she lied, glancing away from him before he saw the lie in her face. An alarming shade of red crept from her neck to the tops of her ears as her eyes continued to dart around the room.

He rolled his eyes. "Make sure she gets to rest," he said, glancing at me with disgust. "She needs to be healed and ready for viewing in two weeks."

She nodded, but as she did, Hunter's voice drifted through the room again, causing Belinda to jerk. "Murdering bitch," he said as she whimpered. She struggled to her feet, stumbling a few steps forward before straightening.

"What's wrong with you?" Jim asked, raising a brow. I frowned, trying to understand why Hunter was accusing her of murder again. I couldn't imagine that he was lying. My stomach churned in warning.

Who did she kill?

"I guess I'm just jumpy with a dead body in the house," she said, still glancing around the room. Her body shivered as she hugged her arms across her stomach. I could sense fear sliding through her. Again, I experienced that satisfaction I felt earlier... That sense of justice.

"As long as that's all it is," Jim said, his eyes roaming over her in suspicion. Another fear caused her to straighten... Fear of Jim... Fear of torture... Fear of death.

She straightened before swallowing, her hand twisting the hem of her shirt as she forced her gaze to meet his. "Of course, it is."

"Get cleaned up, Shayla," he said, barely looking at me as he scrutinized Belinda's face, deciding if she was worth punishment. "And go to bed."

I nodded as I padded to my bathroom. As soon as the door closed, I sighed in relief to be away from them. Still, I wanted to know why Hunter believed Belinda to be a murderer. That warning whispered through my mind, telling me the secret behind the veil may be too much for my fragile mind to handle.

"Hunter?" I whispered. A shiver moved down my spine, telling me he was near.

"I'm here, Shayla," he said softly, his voice charged with worry and anger.

"Why did you call Belinda a murderer?" I asked, tensing because I understood that the reason would break me further.

His sigh echoed through the room. "You've had enough happen tonight," he said, his voice filled with remorse. "Rest, and I will tell you in the morning. I promise."

My heart clenched because at that moment, his tenderness indicated he might really care for me. I swallowed, wondering if I was even more insane for believing him when, just a few hours earlier, he wanted my torture... My death.

"You'll be here in the morning?" I asked, as fear and hope wound through me.

"I'll always be with you," he said, his voice soft. "I will make sure no one hurts you again and those who have, they will face justice."

I nodded, but even if he was telling the truth, he wouldn't be able to protect me all the time. Nobody had ever been able to. People always found a way to break me no matter what, and his protection wouldn't stop them.

Chapter Eleven/ Hunter

I WATCHED SHAYLA SLEEP, grateful that her chest still rose and fell... That her heart still beat in her chest as all the baleful thoughts filled my head twisting within my mind with my love for her that had almost been shattered to pieces because I misinterpreted what was actually happening as I lay dying. I realized now, that my death was another means to keep her trapped with her abusers.

My fingertips skimmed over her cool forehead, but even that caused her to wince away in fear, piercing me with my own guilt and remorse. She was so damn strong but so damn fragile at the same time... Her soul had been splintered so much that one move would break her completely and yet, she still continued to live.

Melancholy sliced through me, damaging me soul-deep. I should have been protecting her from the beginning, not trying to break and kill her. Each torture slid through my mind, punishing me further for harming this woman who was so full of love that she sacrificed herself for another.

A light grew, luminous within the gloomy room. I broke from my study of it, worried that I left her alone to never return, though my energy was still strong, but I found her still sleeping beside me.

I raised my eyes to the cloaked figure who stood within the room, his presence representing the deceitful way he had led me to her.

"What are you doing here?" I asked, angry that he didn't tell me of her innocence and had only given me a cryptic message as a clue.

"The path had a twist in it to bring you here," he said in that raspy voice of his. "The one who harmed has become the protector."

My nostrils flared because again, he continued to speak in riddles. A turbulent storm rose within me. It felt dangerous to me and, if it was dangerous to me, it was dangerous to her. "I'll ask you again... What are you doing here?"

"A soul came to us... Dark... Evil," he said, his raspy voice cutting through me. "So dark the city has lightened because it no longer resides here."

"He tried to rape Shayla," I whispered, afraid to wake her. "He had already beaten her by the time I arrived."

The being's cloak twitched. "He was going to kill her," he stated with no emotion in his voice, but the words caused the storm in me to churn even more. "I was called to reap her soul. You gave me his instead."

The thought of Shayla dead struck through me, and I was glad I had killed him, if only so she continued to breathe...to live.

"So, you're a reaper?" I asked, narrowing my eyes because I understood fully that any souls I collected would be his.

"Yes," he said, the shadow of his chin touching his cloak. "But I also seek justice. Only the souls of those who have done wrong benefit me. Her soul was innocent and would do no good for what I need to accomplish."

"Why didn't you tell me of her innocence?" I asked, gritting my teeth. "Why didn't you tell me who she was?"

"You must find the guilty for yourself," he said, his hood twitching again. "We must find you worthy."

I didn't know who the 'we' were he referred to. I only knew him, and he was pissing me off. I took a deep breath, trying to calm myself. "I don't care if I'm worthy as long as she's safe," I whispered, my soul aching with love and guilt, affection and remorse.

"For you to remain with her... You must be found worthy," he said, causing me to jerk as understanding registered within me. "Bring me more darkened souls. Lighten this city before it crumbles. The more tortured they are by their sins when they pass, the more the city lightens. Give them guilt. Torture them with it. Then, send them to us."

I opened my mouth to ask more questions, but the reaper had already faded, leaving me alone with Shayla. To remain with her, to protect her... I would have to kill again. It was a good thing I had already planned on killing anyone who had or would hurt her.

SHE AWOKE SLOWLY. HER eyes squeezed shut as the light played across her face, illuminating each bruise, each physical trauma. She moaned, a soft exhale, filled with her exhaustion and pain. Her movements were stiff as she reached up to stretch, but stopped when she winced. Only then did she open her green eyes.

"Hunter," my name falling from her lips surprised me and I stiffened as my eyes traveled to her face.

"I'm here," I whispered, my fragile hope that she could forgive me rose in my soul. "I can show myself if you want."

Her eyes widened, that awful fear rippling through their emerald surfaces. "No," she whispered, her bottom lip trembling. "Please... Give me time to face that you're here this way."

Heartache tore through me. I would do anything to make her comfortable with me. If that meant I could only speak to her, and not show my form to her, for the rest of her life, it would have to be enough.

"It's okay, Shayla," I said, softly. "I won't show myself unless I need to, and I'll tell you to close your eyes."

She nodded, a frown creating a v in the center of her forehead. "You wanted to kill me yesterday, but you want to protect me now. Why?"

Dark guilt rose in me, and I sighed. "When I touch you, I see your memories. At first, I thought you ordered my death or were the cause of it, because as I died, Jim called for you so you could see what you caused. Those were his words."

"I didn't order it," she said, a tear slipping down her pale, bruised face. "But I *am* the reason. If I hadn't tried to leave... To gain my freedom, Jim wouldn't have come for Desi. If he wouldn't have come for Desi, you would still be alive."

Anger burned through me as caustic as acid, but it wasn't toward her. All her abusers had made her believe she didn't deserve freedom, and if she tried to achieve it, anything that happened to prevent her from breaking free from her prison was her fault. I had even been guilty of punishing her for those things.

"It's not your fault, Shayla," I said, my voice tight. "It's Jim's fault for killing me... For hurting Desi. It's your stepmother's for allowing them to harm you when she should have protected you and it's everyone's fault who hides their sins behind Jim. It's even mine because I thought the worst of you when you had done nothing wrong. But I was the one who was wrong. You are the last person who should be blamed."

"I don't deserve freedom," she said, tears falling faster down her face.

"Yes. You do," I choked out. "When I touch you, I see your memories. At first, they were flashes which only showed you watching when Desi was hurt. But then I saw the whole nightmarish scene when you cried yesterday. You fought for her. You gave up everything for her. You were selfless. When I touch your tears, I feel exactly what you're feeling. I know you love her more than your freedom. You saved her. You don't deserve punishment. You deserve to be saved, like you saved Desi. I will make everyone pay who has touched you. I will protect you from anyone who tries to harm you. You will be free one day. I'm going to make sure of it."

She opened her mouth to reply, but the door opened, and Belinda stumbled in. Her eyes focused on Shayla, and I stood from my spot beside her, ready to face the next soul marked for the reapers.

The reaper's words slid through my mind as I stalked the woman like prey, *The more tortured they are by their sins, the more the city lightens.*

I zeroed in with a single-minded focus on the woman before me, determined to make the city so bright it would seem as if it had been lit on fire before I was done and I was going to start with Shayla's first torturer. Belinda would face me. Then... she would face the reaper.

Chapter Twelve/ Shayla

I LISTENED TO HUNTER, my body relaxing as his voice soothed me, healing the animosity from the day before. His insistence that I held no guilt sank into my soul, but the insidious voice in the back of my mind was still insisting I take some of the responsibility for his death and Desi's pain. I couldn't help but to return to the fact that if they had never met me, Desi wouldn't have been hurt and Hunter wouldn't be dead.

My peace abated when he offered to show himself. The minatory image of him choking me flashed through my mind. I shivered.

Though he no longer seemed angry with me, fear of deceit crept through me. I worried he might be tricking me, luring me into trusting him, so that he could hurt me more. But his words were pushing my guilt away. It was a refreshing reprieve. But if I saw him, I was afraid of what I would see. I didn't want to lose the version of Hunter currently in my head. I didn't want to shatter the illusion.

If I saw him, that voice telling me it was my fault because they met me would get louder.

Remembering his vengeance might send me over the edge of sanity right now, and I couldn't afford the risk. But I wasn't sure I could trust his newfound kindness.

He had sworn to gain my freedom, but I had ignored it. I feared even hoping for freedom. I was afraid to try again, because Jim would find a way to punish me. He would find a way to harm those I loved and, though Hunter had died, Desi still lived and I didn't want her in danger.

Belinda stopped me from begging him not to try when she came into the room. Her thin lips were curled into a sneer as she stared at me in contempt.

"Hello, Princess," she slurred, her glassy eyes narrowing as she peered at me.

I sensed a shift and realized that Hunter had moved. A chill slid down my spine as I remembered what he had called her the night before... *Murderer.*

"Why are you here?" I asked, wincing as I shifted. I stared at her, wondering how much more pain she came to offer.

"To bring you your pills," she said, a muscle twitching beneath one of her brown eyes as she raised a white bag from the pharmacy down the street. One of the pharmacists there often bid on me and had found a way to give Jim any medicines I needed. "Jim insists you take them."

"What kind of pills?" I asked, looking at the bag suspiciously. After eating her food and becoming sick, I had learned to question anything she gave me.

"Pain pills because the little princess can't handle pain," she sneered, disgust coloring her voice.

The room instantly became colder. Goosebumps broke out on my skin, and I crossed my arms over my chest, trying to push away the chill rippling through the room. I frowned, knowing instinctively that Hunter was the one who caused it.

"Murdering bitch," his words trenchant in the surrounding air, causing that spasmodic twitch beneath her eye to move even more. Her bottom lip trembled as she glanced around the room with wide, panicked eyes.

A sense that I shouldn't react to Hunter slid through me, but unlike the night before, it wasn't because of the satisfaction of justice. There was something dangerous to admitting I had heard him too... Something that made me fear a painful, bloody end that would silence me forever.

"Did you... Hear something?" she asked, her eyes widening so much they bulged.

I frowned and shook my head. "No. Did you?"

"N-No," she said, taking a step away from me. "I-I didn't."

"So, you're a lying, murderous bitch," Hunter's voice echoed through the room. Belinda's hands trembled so much she dropped the pills.

I raised my brow. "Are you alright?" I asked, false concern in my voice as she bent to pick up the bag and tossed it on the bed.

"Just take those," she snapped, turning as she tried to appear normal.

"You can run but you won't escape what you've done," Hunter's voice echoed through the room. Fear painted her face as she paused and glanced around the room. Her back was straight, but her body visibly trembled.

She moved toward the door, stepping beyond it and slamming it behind her so hard a picture fell from the wall. Her heavy footfalls echoed to my room from the stairs before the front door opened and shut.

"She's gone for a while... Probably to drink away the voices," Hunter said, his voice softer. He chuckled darkly. "It won't help her though. This voice will always return."

I frowned, sensing him move closer. "Why won't it help her? Why are you doing this?"

The surrounding air became heavy. Though I could not see him, I sensed his reluctance. "You want to know why I call her a murderer?"

"I do," I said, but as soon as I said it, I wondered if I really wanted to know. There was a peace in ignorance that would be shattered once he told me.

"Remember when I said that I saw your memories when we touched?" He asked on a sigh that was so weighted it settled on my shoulders, pressing hard enough that I had trouble breathing.

I nodded, afraid to speak. Still, he hesitated, and I felt the bed shift as he sat next to me.

"Shayla, what I'm going to tell you will hurt, but I want you to understand she will pay for what she's done," he whispered, remorse clear in his voice.

"Did she kill my dad?" I asked, shaking my head because he had died in a car accident caused by his drunk driving. I couldn't imagine how she would have done that.

"No," he said, his voice rippling with grief. "She hired someone to kill your mother."

All the breath left me as my world spun. "No," I whispered, shaking my head as tears fell from my eyes, but even as I said it, the truth was plain in his words. My mother had been raped and killed during a home robbery. Her death was why my father had become an alcoholic and drug addict. He had loved her so much before he died that he became a ghost of the laughing, kind man he had once been. Three years after her death, he married Belinda out of loneliness and a need for someone to care. Sadly, his addictions became progressively worse after marrying her... and I suspect he felt guilty for marrying Belinda... Like he was betraying my mom. I narrowed my eyes as I realized she had killed him too, because she was the reason for his grief.

"Shayla, I'm sorry," he whispered as my hair moved and I realized he was moving a strand from my face with a measure of care I hadn't received since my mother's death.

"Why?" I whispered and then began to sob as I repeated. "Why?"

"She wanted your father, and he loved your mother," he said so softly I had to strain my ears to understand. "He didn't even notice her because he was so in love with your mother. With her out of the way, her chances were much better."

Visions of what my life would have been like if my mother had not died drifted through my mind, and I was angry... So angry... Becoming angrier still as I realized my mother's death would go unpunished in this town because it was corrupt with people filled with evil intentions. I gritted my teeth because I knew I wanted Belinda to pay for what she had done to my sweet, loving mother and my once loving father. Tears burned my cheeks as I continued to sob.

"I can never apologize enough for believing the worst of you or for the things I have done because of that mistake," Hunter whispered, his words drifting through the air. "But I can promise to give you and your mother the justice you deserve."

I took a shaky breath. "What are you saying?"

There was silence, heavily weighted and twisting with shadows. "What I was going to do to you, is now what I'm going to do to her except this time, I'm sure she truly deserves it," he said, his voice cold enough that I should have been afraid but oddly, I wasn't. He continuously offered the only solace I had found in years in the form of dark, dark promises. "I'm going to make sure she loses her sanity and then I'm going to take her life."

An image of my mother's smile drifted through my mind again and slowly, I nodded because it was the only way that Belinda was going to stand in front of justice and be condemned for her sins. If I was going to be punished and I went to hell for wanting her death, I would gladly stand in the flames for all eternity.

Chapter Thirteen/ Hunter

THE ENIGMA OF DEATH doesn't end when you close your eyes that final time and take that final labored breath. Instead, the mystery of it lasts for eternity... At least for me.

I didn't move on to another place where peace or apathy ruled, nor did I experience any form of indifference or punishment for my 'so–called sins'. Instead, I felt every emotion to a heightened degree that kept the sense of atrophy at bay. Not once did I feel that presence that my mother revered and had prayed to in hopes of making life a little safer... a little better. Maybe he was up there, but he still remained a mystery to me, hiding behind a mist and giving me only the reaper as the singular being that met me in my afterlife.

All I knew was the place where I existed now and the feelings that ruled my actions. In all honesty, my strongest emotion wasn't anger or vengeance. It was a complete love for Shayla and the protectiveness that came with it was fierce. As she slept, I knew I would never allow anyone to hurt her again. I would rid her of those who did. I would punish them for their sins against her–and there were a lot of sins.

When her stepmother stumbled through the front door, I moved out of the room where Shayla lay sleeping. I focused on beginning her torture so I could finally rid Shayla of her presence. As I walked down the stairs, I found her mumbling to herself, incoherent with the scent of wine and whiskey coating her breath so strongly that it seemed to infuse with every molecule in the air.

I let her step inside. She stumbled her way to the couch too inebriated to make it to her room up the stairs without risking falling and breaking her neck. My lips twitched because if she was still worried about her safety, she would still worry about losing her life.

I leaned close, trying to ignore the rancid scent coming from her. "Did you think drinking away your past would rid you of me, murderer?" I asked. She froze, then slowly straightened, trying to hide the shiver taking control of her body, giving away her fear.

Her eyes darted around the room wildly, searching for any reasonable explanation for the disembodied voice she heard yet again. Her body shook, and she paled considerably. Her lips twitched as her chin quivered.

"What's wrong?" I hissed so close to her ear that she started. Gooseflesh rose on her arms. "Do you think you're going crazy, murderer?"

Her eyes widened so far that they seemed as if they would pop out of her head. "I've never killed anybody."

Her words were still slurred, but two tears dropped from her eyes. Maybe she thought I would have sympathy for her but no. After all, how many tears had she caused Shayla to cry? How many did Ellie cry before her death? "No, but you had someone else do it."

Her eyes narrowed as I spoke. "Leonard sent you," she said, gritting her teeth. "There's a walkie-talkie or radio or something around here. He wants more money to keep his mouth shut."

I remained silent for a few minutes, weighing my options as I realized I now had the first name of the man who raped and killed Shayla's mother. I could make him pay too if I could make her panic enough to bring him here.

"Yes," I said, deciding exactly what I was going to do. "Call him and this can end."

It was a lie but an effective one as she picked up the phone and dialed a number. Her face was now flushed with anger. "Leonard," she snapped as a male's voice echoed through the line. "If you want more money, come over."

Thankfully, she didn't accuse him of being the reason for the voices. If she had, he would have denied it and blown my ruse. The man must not have heard the distress in her voice, or he didn't care. "I'll be there."

He didn't ask any questions. It was short and sweet, and then he hung up. Belinda began to rock back and forth. The minutes ticked away in a synchronized illusion of forever as we waited for that knock. Shayla still slept in the safety of her bed above us, clueless to what was going on the floor beneath her.

The knock that came was soft, and I realized he had visited more than once, probably while Shayla was here. But she had never known her mother's rapist and murderer was beneath the same roof as she was. I wondered for a moment how many jobs Belinda had paid him for, or if he just came demanding more money. I suppose it didn't matter because it would end for him tonight. There was a certain headiness to knowing that he would never harm anyone else ever again.

When Belinda tripped over to the door and opened it, I followed her, finding the same man who had taken Ellie Bell's picture... The same man who had done unmentionable deeds to her before killing her. Age had not been kind to him. Rotting teeth lined his mouth and long, scraggly hair that looked like it hadn't been washed for weeks hung from his head. The scent of chemicals drifted to me... A tale-tale sign he was on drugs.

"You have another job?" Leonard asked, licking his parched lips. Most likely, he was itching for a fix and had blown through any money Belinda had previously paid him.

Belinda narrowed her eyes. "I know what you're doing, Leonard," she slurred, shaking a thick finger in his direction. "You set up a radio in here to make me think I was haunted. I didn't think you were smart enough to pull off some shit like this."

"What the fuck are you talking about, woman?" he asked, his brows furrowing as confusion slid through his glassy eyes.

Belinda faltered, her mouth opening and closing before finding her voice. "The voice... You planted something so I would hear the voice so you could get more money."

He shook his head. "I don't know what the hell you are talking about." Leonard's confusion drifted between them. Belinda stumbled back a step. "I've not done anything to you."

I stepped forward, tired of playing with her. The reaper would get one, to terrify the other.

"Murderers," I said, my words drifting over both of them, causing them both to jerk.

"What the fuck was that?" Leonard asked, his eyes going wide.

"If it's not you, you told someone," Belinda said as her body jerked spasmodically.

"Are you crazy?" Leonard asked, his voice rising. "That would put me in prison."

"Murderers of Ellie Bell," I said, my voice falling around them like an anchor as they both fell silent. Tears fell down Belinda's cheeks. Narrowing my eyes, I reached out to allow one to move through me. It held Indignance, anger, and grief, but no guilt. She was far from ready to be killed. I wanted her guilt.

I turned to the man who did the deed and saw him shaking. A single tear fell from his eye. I caught it finding fear, remorse, guilt and shame. A wicked smile slid across my face, finding him ready as I punched through his chest and grabbed his heart. I witnessed every sin he had committed. At first, he did it because he enjoyed it, but he kept doing it because of his addiction. He had been his own punisher, experiencing guilt and then killing it with a high he had gained by committing more atrocities. The cycle had been repeated for years.

"It's time to meet justice, Leonard," I said, as I squeezed the beating muscle that allowed him to live, tighter and tighter. He stiffened and grabbed his chest, his face turning red, gasping for air.

"Leonard!" Belinda's shrill screams moved through the room. "What's happening?"

"Exactly what will happen to you but first you will lose everything... First, you will lose your sanity," I gritted out as Leonard gasped his final breath and his soul left his body. It slammed into my chest as my soul became the gateway for him to join the reapers. His body fell at my feet.

Belinda went to her knees beside him, her body trembling as she touched his neck. She jerked back, finding no pulse. "You will meet your end, Belinda, but your death will be much more painful. But I promise, in the end, you will meet justice for all you have done."

I pushed Belinda away from the body. She stumbled and fell before moving through the kitchen and living room, taking the energy from the lights and causing them to shutter and spark, I moved upstairs to Shayla's room where I would protect her until she woke, and I could tell her one of her mother's murderers was dead.

Chapter Fourteen/
Shayla

VENGEANCE... IT WAS such an odd word... One that evoked images of people hiding in alleys dressed in black, with knives or guns, awaiting those who did them wrong. It was a word cloaked in darkness, almost synonymous with evil, but as my eyes opened fresh from a dream of my mother's funeral, vengeance took on a new meaning. It became a path to peace... A path to justice.

I sat up in bed, wincing at the soreness in my muscles as I stood, seemingly alone, but I sensed I wasn't. Hunter's voice echoed through the room, confirming that.

"Be careful as you move, Shayla," Hunter's voice drifted to me from near the door. "But I want you to come and listen. Something happened while you slept."

I didn't speak. I was afraid to, as I moved toward his voice and cracked open the door. My body tensed as Belinda's shaky voice reached up to the stairs to where I stood. "Jim?"

I tensed, not wanting to face him if he was here. The thought of him touching me made my stomach churn. Hunter's presence calmed me.

"Why are you calling, Belinda?" He snapped, and I sighed in relief, realizing that he was on the phone on speaker as I opened my door further.

My eyes widened as I peered over the landing, jumping back toward my door. There was a man lying beside the front entrance. A dark knowing settled in the pit of my stomach as I realized he was dead.

"Stay here," Hunter said, near my ear.

I nodded as Belinda spoke again and I sensed his presence move farther away from me, but I was too focused on Belinda's conversation with Jim to question what Hunter was doing.

"I have a problem," she said, speaking in a voice so low that I had to strain to understand her.

There was a pause on the line before Jim spoke. "Is Shayla okay?" He asked, as if he cared about me more than an object to be bought and sold. I rolled my eyes because I knew better than that. Jim only cared about using my body and the money it brought him.

"Y-Yes," Belinda said, her voice cracking. "She's asleep but—"

"Then why are you calling me?" Jim asked, his voice tinged with anger.

"Th-There's a dead body on my living room floor," she whispered, but I was still able to hear it.

"Is he one of my... associates?" Jim asked, his voice near snapping.

Belinda remained silent for a long period. "No," she said, choking on her words. "He's connected to me."

"Then it sounds like it's your mess," Jim hissed angrily. "You need to clean it up."

"But—"

"There are no buts, Belinda," he said, his voice lethal even through the phone. "But I will warn you, be discreet. You don't want to find out what happens if you aren't."

Belinda gasped, almost choking on her fear as the line went silent. Hunter's laughter echoed through the apartment.

"It sounds like you are on your own, Belinda," he said, spitting her name out as if it were a curse. "It's funny how criminals turn their backs on you when they no longer need you. I wonder how long it will be before he decides to put you in the ocean?"

Belinda's sobs traveled through the apartment. "Have fun cleaning up your mess," Hunter chuckled. "It will be the least of your troubles when I'm through with you."

Belinda sobbed as I had many times over the years. I closed my eyes, savoring the sound of her facing the same emotions she had evoked in me. I stepped back into my room, closing my door and made my way to my bed. I sank down onto the mattress. Scattered emotions rolled through me, making me want to laugh and cry at the same time. I closed my eyes, wondering if I was going insane.

The gentle sweep of my hair from my face made me open my eyes but finding no one standing in front of me was disconcerting.

"Hunter," I whispered, glancing around the room for another clue he was there.

"I'm here, Shayla," he said, his voice gentle in a way I had never experienced.

"Can you show yourself?" I asked, hoping that seeing him would make me saner.

"Won't you be afraid?" he asked, his worry sinking into me.

"No," I sighed. He had already shown me he didn't mean me harm. "I thought you were still trying to hurt me before. I won't be afraid now."

Complete silence answered me, but somehow, I sensed he was still nearby. Then, so low I almost didn't hear it, he said, "Okay."

A shimmer of light moved in front of me before I found myself gazing into his beautiful blue eyes. I reached out to him but, as suspected, my hands skimmed through him. I gave him a sad smile.

"It must suck not to experience a touch," I whispered, my eyes tearing.

"I am able to," he said, taking a deep breath. "I feel you more than I would be able to if I were alive."

"Because you can see my memories?" I asked, wondering if he had captured anything from my touch this time.

"Yes, and I feel your emotions," he said, his lips twitching into a smile. "I had to guess those things when I was alive."

"I guess you realize what I want to know then," I whispered as he sat down beside me.

He nodded, his smile fading. "The man who died tonight was the man who killed your mother. Yes, I killed him, but he deserved his death... He deserved much more."

I tensed as a tremble slid through me. My mother's face flashed to the front of my memory as a tear trickled down my cheek.

"I promised you justice," Hunter said, softly. "I'm keeping that promise no matter how dark that justice may be."

I swallowed my grief and raised my eyes to Hunter's, wishing he could wrap me in his embrace. He reached forward to cup my cheek, and I experienced the same love I had always experienced when I thought of him move through me, along with a sense of great sadness. I knew he felt the same for me, but those feelings could never develop into a normal relationship. That possibility had been stolen from us.

"I realize I can't give you what you need from me," he said, his eyes darkening as he took in my emotions. "It's not fair."

I shook my head as the grief of his death hit me again. "No, it's not."

He leaned forward and pressed his lips against mine. I inhaled sharply because I could feel him just as much as I felt his first kiss. He moved away from me.

"You kissed me," I whispered, tears falling down my cheeks as my heart ached with so much love for him. "And I felt it. Just like my first kiss."

He shrugged. "You were crying," he said, his eyes tender. "You remember, my dad always kissed my mom when she cried to make her feel better?"

I laughed, chasing away some of the melancholy. "You still use that line?" I asked. He grinned. "How many girls have you kissed because they cried?"

His grin widened. "Truthfully?"

"Truthfully," I said, raising my brow.

"One girl with two names," he said, a sigh breaking from between his lips. "The first time, she told me her name was Ellie and the second time, I found out her name was Shayla and though I have kissed a few more girls than her, it was never because they cried and I wanted to make them feel better. She was also the only girl I ever searched for afterwards."

My heart thudded in my chest as I took in his words. "You looked for me?"

He nodded slowly, "Every single day since that day at the beach," he whispered, his voice drenching me in lost opportunities.

"Why would you look for me?" I asked, frowning.

His fingertips moved over my cheek, leaving a streak of icy cold behind. "You weren't the only one to get their first kiss that day," he said, his eyes meeting mine. "I admit I may have schemed a bit to make it happen, but I wanted it because there was something about you that made me want to protect you and keep you. I understand love at first sight, sounds cheesy, but meeting you was a warm, precious moment that I remembered every day. The only explanation I can give you is that I loved you from the moment I met you."

I sighed; my heart heavy. "I understand exactly how you feel," I whispered. "Because I've loved you from that day, too."

"I know," he said, his eyes shining with affection and heartbreak. "I experienced it in your tears."

He leaned forward and kissed my forehead. I closed my eyes as I sank further into our dark, twisted love that would never have a happily ever after.

Chapter Fifteen/ Hunter

I WATCHED SHAYLA SLEEP, mesmerized by her chest rising and falling as her breaths moved from between her parted lips. Each breath was more precious to me than anything I accomplished in life. Still, I ached to hold her... to keep her safe, to give her the warmth of my body as she listened to my heart beating against her ear. Bitter pain moved through me because I wanted to give her everything. I wanted to hold her hand, touch her without the veil of death between us. I wanted to be seen with her. None of those things could ever happen.

I touched her cheek. She moved unconsciously toward me, her body seeking my touch as she curled up next to me. My soul trembled with light and darkness twirling together until I kissed her forehead, only straightening when I sensed someone else enter the apartment. Voices moved up the stairwell, and I stood, stepping out of the room, pulling energy from the lights as I traveled down the stairs.

"How did he die?" A man asked, his voice familiar in the shadows of the living room. A chill slid through my consciousness. I had been in this man's presence before.

"What does it matter?" Belinda hissed, "If he's found, there will be questions, and those questions will lead back to me, Jim, and then you."

"Are you threatening us, Belinda?" The man asked, stepping further into the room and standing under the light. I gritted my teeth, recognizing one of the goons who had held me as Jim took my life.

"I'm not threatening you, Mick," Belinda said, raising her chin, her beady eyes sparking with defiance. "I'm asking for assistance in ridding both of us of a problem... One that will only cause more problems as time passes if he is found here."

"What did Jim say when you called him?" He asked, raising a brow and crossing his arms over his barrel chest.

"He told me to take care of it," she said, not lying for once. "And that's what I'm trying to do... Take care of it."

"So, it is no problem of mine," Mick said, turning his back on her as he shrugged his shoulders. "Jim doesn't want it taken care of by us, and since he's my boss, I must listen to him or face dire, dire consequences."

"What can I give you?" Belinda asked, her voice edging with desperation as Mick turned back to her with a raised brow. She glanced toward Shayla's room. I narrowed my eyes as I understood exactly what she was offering, but Mick laughed.

"Money," he said, shaking his head before rolling his eyes. "I can have her anytime I want. It's one of the perks of working for Jim."

My nostrils flared as he talked about violating Shayla as casually as if he were discussing a car payment. I turned and moved up the stairs, deciding that he would be the next to die, but to do that, I would have to leave Shayla alone. Too many dead bodies in her apartment may make Shayla a suspect, and I wouldn't allow that.

When I made it to Shayla's room, I touched her cheek. "Shayla," I whispered. She opened her eyes, searching for me as her body tensed. I appeared in front of her and she relaxed. "I'm going to be gone for less than an hour. Keep your door locked and don't let anyone in. I will be back very soon."

"What are you doing?" she asked, her voice still husky from sleep. Her brow furrowed.

"Do you know Mick?" I asked, and she immediately paled, flinching at the sound of his name. Anger lit through me because Shayla always had to fear everyone in her life.

She nodded. "H-He's one of the men who helps Jim," she said, a tremble working over her body. "H-He's one of his bodyguards. Sometimes, he gives the punishments Jim orders."

"Not after tonight," I said, reaching forward and touching her cheek, hoping she could feel me enough to give her some peace. "I promise... He'll never harm you or anyone else again."

A breath moved from between her lips and relief fell over her features, making me wonder how many times the vile man had hurt her.

"I'll lock the door," she said as I bent to kiss her forehead.

She rose, following me as I moved into the hallway. I stayed still until I heard the click of the lock and then hurried down the stairs. Mick was balancing Lawrence's body over his shoulder and heading into the garage where he had parked. I watched, impatiently, as he lowered the body in the trunk of the shiny black car and turned to Belinda.

"He'll be taken care of," he said as he took the money she held in her hand and tucked it into the breast pocket of his jacket, "But keep it between me and you. If Jim said it was your problem, he may be less than pleased that I intervened."

"It's our little secret," Belinda said, but no smile moved upon her lips.

Mick nodded and got into the car. I smiled when I realized he didn't put on his seatbelt. I slipped into the passenger seat, awaiting my time... His time.

The garage opened, and he backed out. I heard a noise behind us and turned to see the door closing as he exited the driveway. Two miles passed in silence before he turned west, and I realized he was driving toward the beach. Thoughts rolled through my head as I considered options on the path to his death. He would never make it. Not only that, but his death would also be devastating to Belinda and Jim.

I focused on the street well ahead of us, my body pulsing before I closed my eyes. When I opened them, I was well ahead of him, standing on the road, his car fast approaching. I pulled energy from the streetlights on either side. Their bulbs burst in a shower of sparks over me as I made myself visible. The headlights washed over me and through me, illuminating my apparition causing me to glow.

Mick was glancing down but the moment he raised his head, his eyes widened, and he pulled sharply on the wheel. The car careened off the road and slammed into one of the light poles. Steam rose from the crushed metal of the hood.

He had been going so fast that his body flew through the windshield, shattering glass around him as he landed on the hood with a bone crushing thud. Blood fell from his face, now gashed and mangled, with pieces of glass embedded in his skin. A groan moved from his lips as I stepped beside him. His eyes opened and moved to my face, causing a strangled cry to break from him and blood to bubble from his lips.

"Remember me?" I asked, moving closer, my face a mask of all the rage and anger coursing through my soul.

"D-Dead... Y-You're dead," he gasped, struggling for breath as his face turned crimson.

My nostrils flared as a smile moved over my face. "So are you or you will be," I said with a sardonic smile.

"I'm sorry," he said, gasping.

"I don't care," I said, reaching into his body and gripping his heart, the weakened pulse barely trembling on my palm even before I tightened my fist. He gasped and, though I would have loved to draw out his torture, his death was as quick as the guilt flowing through him with his last breath. His soul left his body to become the property of the reaper.

I walked away from the scene, smiling because he was known as Jim's bodyguard and now, he was dead with the corpse of a criminal in the trunk... A criminal Belinda was supposed to get rid of.

I chuckled as I wondered how Jim would explain all of this, but more importantly, I wondered how he was going to punish Belinda for involving his bodyguard in the cleanup she was supposed to take care of. I closed my eyes, focusing on Shayla as I pulled energy from everything I could around me. The energy flooded my soul, which flickered as I joined her with the news that Mick would never harm her or anyone else again.

Chapter Sixteen/ Shayla

SILENCE... IT HAS ALWAYS unnerved me, but as I waited for Hunter to return, the silence brought only the sound of my breaths rushing in and out of my lungs, becoming quicker and harsher with each moment. Thoughts rushed through my head... Unbidden and unwanted... Thoughts of what would come with my death. Was I going to go to hell? Would I burn forever in the pits of lava with the same people who had harmed me?

I swallowed hard over the lump in my throat as a tear trekked down my cheek. The worry truly terrified me, as every deed I had done and every lie I had spoken moved into my soul, staining me further. My lips trembled because I realized, even with the immanence of burning in the eternal flames in the bowels of hell, I couldn't feel guilty for the death of the man who had raped and murdered my mother, nor could I find remorse for Mick as I awaited his killer to return. Yet, I cried because I found it unfair that I risked hell for wanting to rid the world of these evil people. It wasn't fair because they deserved worse than death.

Hunter's hand on my cheek announced his arrival and shattered those thoughts as my tears fell through his hand. His gaze was a caress to me and as much as I was glad that those two men had died, I desperately wished Hunter was still alive.

"Shayla," Hunter whispered, sitting on the bed next to me. Though the bed didn't move as his body fell next to mine, he was more present to me than anyone had ever been.

"Is there a hell?" I asked, causing his brow to furrow. He must be aware. He must have faced... Something after death.

He gave me a sad smile. "I have no idea where other souls go," he said, tilting his head. " I didn't see hell, but I didn't see heaven either."

His eyes moved over me, concern marked his brow. My darkness was reflected in his eyes. "Is Mick dead?" I asked, wishing Hunter had a better answer. He stared at me for a few moments in silence before he nodded.

"He won't be hurting you anymore," he said softly.

"I'm glad," I sighed before taking a shaky breath.

"That's the problem, isn't it?" He asked, lying next to me. He turned to face me. "The guilt isn't because Mick died. The guilt is because you're not experiencing sadness over his death and you think it makes you a bad person."

"No, not bad," I said, my heart clenching. "Damned. I'm afraid I'm damned."

Hunter reached up and brushed my hair from my face. "I have no idea if there is a hell and I don't know if there is a heaven," he said, softly. "But I do know that if there is a heaven, you deserve to be there. You're not bad, Shayla. You're the best person I know."

"I don't want heaven either," I said, my heart clenching with the love I had for him.

"What do you want, Shayla?" He asked, raising his brow.

"I want to be with you," I said, reaching forward to touch him, but my hand slid through him. "When I die, I want to be with you. Whether that's in heaven or hell or somewhere in between, that's where I want to be."

"And I'll fight for you to be with me," he said, sighing.

The silence stretched again, and I was beginning to feel the pressure of it falling on me and stealing the peace I had with Hunter near. "How did Mick die?" I asked, more to break the nothingness in the air.

"I squeezed his heart until it quit beating after he flew through the windshield of his wrecked car," he said, his face emotionless.

"Did it hurt?" I asked, trying not to drown in the shame of knowing that I wanted it to. Images floated through my mind, marking all the horrible things he had done to me, and I wanted him to hurt before he had died.

Hunter caressed my cheek. He froze, and his nostrils flared. "Yes, but I should have tortured him more."

I shifted on the bed. "Did you just see... everything he did to me?" I asked as shame slid through me. I hated that Hunter had witnessed those moments of weakness with a touch.

He nodded, taking a deep breath. "But he won't hurt you again," he said, gritting his teeth. "Though his death will have consequences for Belinda and Jim."

I frowned as I took in his face. "What do you mean?"

"Belinda was supposed to take care of the body herself," he said, frowning. "But she involved Mick. Mick died with a dead man's body in his trunk, and he was Jim's bodyguard. Jim will have to cover that up, and Belinda will suffer for it."

"It sounds like Belinda will get the worst of it," I said, because Jim rarely suffered consequences for the things he did. He always found a way to get away with his sins.

Hunter's finger traced along my jaw. "He will face the consequences of his actions. If there is no hell, I will make one here for him before he dies."

"You're going to drive him crazy like Belinda?" I asked, trying to imagine him suffering but unable to bring it to my mind. Nobody had hurt me more than he had. He deserved to suffer horribly.

"It won't be like Belinda," Hunter said, shaking his head.

"What do you mean?" I asked, my eyes tracing over his face.

"I'm driving her crazy with my presence," he said, shrugging,

"And she'll find out I'm at fault for Mick's death. She witnessed the death of your mom's murderer, and I taunted her with it, but Jim will watch everyone who has been part of his sins fall dead around him until there is just him. He will start seeing me everywhere and when I speak to him, his sanity will be gone. Only then will I give him a slow, painful death. When he dies, this city will be spotless."

I stared at him, taking him in with my mouth hanging open. The thought of Jim gone from this world made my heart leap.

"I'm glad he will die that way," I said as my heart sank. "Though the city will be washed clean, I will never be spotless. I'll always remember everything he did. His death and torture are the only fitting payment."

"None of us are spotless in life, Shayla," Hunter said, kissing my forehead. "All of us have darkness. All of us have pain. That doesn't mean anything. The thing that means the most is the ability to still love, the will to survive and the heart to stand up and be brave. Those are the purest things in the world, and you have them, Shayla. So, no...You're not spotless, but you are pure in the things that count."

I smiled as my eyes began to grow heavy and the weight in my heart lifted. "Will you stay with me?"

"As long as you want me to," Hunter said, his breath against my ear.

"Forever... That's how long I want you to stay, Hunter," I said, my eyes closing.

"Then, I'm not going anywhere," his lips pressed against my temple as sleep took me into its darkened embrace.

Chapter Seventeen/
Hunter

SHAYLA'S SOFT BREATHING filled the room, her eyes closed in slumber. I studied her, taking in her beautiful face, but my thoughts moved to Belinda and how I would remove her from Shayla's life. My head spun with ideas, rejecting each means of torture, hoping to punish her in ways that would make her remaining days hell on earth.

My rage at the woman in the living room on the floor below us increased as Shayla's breathing accelerated. I straightened. Her body started thrashing., Her hand swiped through me by accident. Images of Belinda traveled quickly through my mind, showing me exactly why Shayla's hair was no longer dark like her mother's had been. Her feelings crashed through me as a tear landed on me... Panic because it was the only thing she had left of her mother. Sadness... Because it was being taken away and fear, that ever-present fear, when Belinda was around her because she constantly wondered what the woman would do next to harm her.

My finger skimmed her cheek. "Don't worry, Shayla," I whispered, pressing my lips against her forehead, putting all the love I felt for her in that kiss. "She will pay for everything she's done. She will know exactly how you have felt all these years. I promise."

Immediately, Shayla calmed, and though I didn't want to leave her, I knew I needed energy again to do what needed to be done. I kissed her one final time, locking her door before moving through it and down the stairs. It was Belinda's car that I pulled energy from this time, draining it completely. I paused a moment to relish that she truly had no easy escape from me before walking back inside.

I found Belinda sleeping peacefully on the couch, an empty bottle of whiskey beside her. My hands curled at my sides, wishing to watch her life fade away beneath my hands. Gritting my teeth, I realized it would be too soon and too merciful to end her life now.

"Sleeping with any sort of peace won't do, Belinda," I whispered quietly before going to the kitchen and finding scissors in the drawer. I stood beside her, taking her in. Her shoulder length dark hair fell over her round, bloated face–bloated from drinking too much alcohol.

"I think you need a haircut," I whispered, picking up the locks and cutting them as close to the scalp as I could, leaving the strands lying around her so they would be the first things she would see when she woke. I left the scissors on the table in front of the couch.

"Belinda," I said in a singsong voice, but she didn't move. She was deep in her drunken stupor.

I glanced at the table and found the television remote. I picked it up and turned the television on, intending to turn up the volume fully to shock her awake. The news came to life on the screen. They were covering Mick's wreck and demise. A cold smile crossed my face. *Perfect.*

I turned it up as loud as it would go. Belinda bolted upright as I placed the remote back on the table.

Her glazed eyes found the screen before widening. "Mick," she whispered as she took in the scene, too shocked to realize she had gotten a new haircut. "No."

"I really wish I could eat popcorn right now," I said. She nearly jumped out of her skin at the sound of my voice. "Too bad you can't do that when you're dead."

"You killed him?" She asked, her words trembling from her lips.

She glanced around the room, her panic rising, flavoring the air as she tried to place where I was.

"A body found in the car has yet to be identified," the announcer said. Her head jerked back toward the television, and she seemed to forget about me for a moment. Her breath rasped from her as a tremor slid over her body.

"Oh yeah, about that... He didn't have enough time to dump the body," I said as her eyes bulged from their sockets. "I wonder if there is a way to trace your dear friend Leonard back to you. Wasn't there a phone call you made right before he came over? It wasn't on a burner, was it?"

"Shut up!" She screamed, closing her eyes tight. A shaky hand moved to her mouth.

"I wonder what Jim is going to think when he hears about this," I whispered in her ear as she pulled in a breath. "Do you think he'll be angry?"

She glanced around in panic as she lowered her hand, closing it in a fist around the strands of hair there. She lowered her gaze. Her mouth opened and closed before reaching up and touching her head, discovering most of her hair was gone. A sob broke from her throat, and I grinned, finding satisfaction in her distress.

"You did this?" she asked, with tears spilling from her eyes down her face.

"Who knows?" I asked, laughing, "Perhaps you're crazy. Perhaps you did it all and imagined me as someone to blame."

"N-No. I didn't. Did I?" she whispered, shaking her head as she picked locks of her hair up, staring at them in despair.

"Well, you ordered Ellie Bell's murder," I said, narrowing my eyes because she couldn't deny that without lying. "You've sold her daughter to men for sex and abused her yourself in other ways. Perhaps you are experiencing a bit of guilt."

She laughed hysterically. "Why would I feel guilty over the things I've done to those bitches? You're fucking real. I don't know how, but you are."

"You're right," I said, grinning. "I am. I am here for your sins. I am here to make you face them. There is no telling what else you've done, but I do intend to find out. When I'm done with you, you'll have no secrets, and you'll have nowhere to hide."

I reached forward and touched her, her memories playing in front of me and rage slid through my veins as hot as a branding iron.

I found a man I assumed was Nick Bell holding his head in his hands as he sat on the couch in a ratty living room. Brown locks spilled over the fingers he had shoved into his hair. Tears flowed from his blue eyes.

"I can't drink anymore," he whispered, closing his eyes tight. "I have to be there for Shayla. I keep waking up to find her crying or with bruises and I can't remember what happened to cause those things. Ellie... Wouldn't want me to be this way. I have to be a dad to her."

"Nick," Belinda said, raising her brow, her voice dripping with false sympathy. "You know you aren't strong enough to do that. You have to have time to forget. Don't worry. I'm here to take care of her."

She walked to the refrigerator, bending to pull out a beer before popping the tab on it and walking back toward him, taking the seat beside him.

"Let me show you that you aren't strong enough to face that grief yet" she said, waving it beneath his nose, causing his eyes to move toward the can. "You want some, don't you?"

He licked his lips and shook his head, closing his eyes, but she pushed it closer to his face. A tear fell down his cheek as he sighed, giving in, grabbing the can and putting it to his lips. His hands were shaking as he gulped down the contents. His eyes bore the torture of his failure.

I released Belinda, my nostrils flaring in rage. She had depressed the man by killing the woman he loved and had then prevented him from breaking his addiction when he could have become a father to Shayla.

I grabbed her by the neck, those images playing through my mind again. "You kept Nick Bell addicted," I said, seething. "He died drinking and driving. You are at fault for his death, too."

"He...would have left...me if he...got clean," she choked out.

I released her, staring down at her with no remorse. "He should have left you," I hissed. "You are a poison infecting everyone around you."

"I...I loved him!" she cried out.

"No, you didn't, and you acted out sin after sin with that excuse, but it was a lie," I said, disgusted that a human such as her could walk on this earth. "But every sin you've committed, you'll pay for. So, you won't die yet, Belinda. A quick, peaceful death is too good for you. You destroyed a family for your selfishness. There will be nothing that will calm you before you close your eyes for the final time. Your hell will continue now. If there is any justice, it will continue afterwards, but you will experience it while you still breathe on this earth."

A key turned in the door and she jerked her head toward it as a sob broke from her throat. The moment I saw who stood there, I smiled, because I realized her torture would continue without me. Jim had arrived and from the expression on his face, he was seething with fury.

Chapter Eighteen/ Shayla

SCREAMS BLENDED FROM my dreams into reality as I sat up in bed, searching the darkness for Hunter. Though he wasn't in the room, I sensed he was somewhere close as I moved toward the door. Another scream echoed through the house, and I frowned when I realized it was Belinda.

I knew that Hunter was probably torturing her again, but a sick curiosity had me unlocking the door and poking my head out. The coast was clear, so I tiptoed to the landing and peered over, but I couldn't see Belinda from where I stood.

I carefully crept down the stairs and peeked into the living room, my eyes widened at the scene that was playing out before me. Hunter was standing in the center of the room with his arms crossed over his chest. Hair lay in chunks on the couch. Belinda was standing near the coffee table, her eyes bloodshot from drunkenness and tears. Her hair was an uneven mess, with chunks cut so close to the scalp I could see the pink skin beneath. Jim stood near her; his face twisted in rage. His two remaining bodyguards flanked him as he stared down at Belinda.

I frowned, confused. "What happened to your hair?"

Belinda's head snapped toward me and Jim turned his head, his eyes raking over my body, taking in the bruises and the pained way I was standing at the entrance to the living room.

"This crazy bitch cut it all off," Jim growled.

Belinda shook her head, tears filling her eyes. "N-No, I didn't," she said, her body trembling. "I-It was—."

"I don't want to hear it!" Jim shouted, raising his chin. "You need to step carefully, Belinda because the only reason you will live through the night is because I don't need to answer questions about the disappearance of someone else acquainted with me. That is, quite frankly, the only thing that's keeping you alive."

Belinda's eyes grew large, her lip trembled as her hand covered her mouth. Jim stepped toward her and gripped her throat. "You are to take care of Shayla. If anything happens to her... Anything... I won't hold back. Do you understand?"

Belinda nodded, her movements shaky.

"Now, I have to clean up your mess with Mick," he said, tightening his grip on her throat.

"Mick?" I asked, realizing I needed to question what had happened or it would seem suspicious.

"He's dead... He died in a car accident tonight cleaning up something I told Belinda to take care of on her own," he hissed, his face red. "Now, the wrong people are asking a lot of questions."

"Mick's dead?" I asked, glancing at Belinda as Jim tightened his grip once more before releasing her. She gasped for breath as she held her throat.

"Yes. He's dead. Because you are my goddaughter, people may arrive to ask you questions," he said, stepping close to me, gripping my chin to pull my face up until my eyes met his. "If they do, they will see you hurt. You need to tell them Mick did this to you and I fired him. Do you understand, Shayla?"

I pulled my chin from his fingers, my stomach twisting because he had touched me.

"I understand."

"Good girl," he said, kissing my forehead. "Go rest. I need you better. I miss you."

I heard Hunter's growl as my stomach twisted. I forced a grateful smile and nodded at Jim.

"I'll go get some rest," I said, backing away before turning and making my way upstairs. I knew that Hunter was following me. His anger pierced through me as I shut the door.

"Hunter," I whispered, turning to find him close. His eyes flashed with an eerie light. His anger was so potent that fear slid down my spine and I backed away.

He closed his eyes. "I'm not going to hurt you, Shayla," he said, opening them. "I will not hurt you again."

"I can sense your anger," I whispered. He nodded, not denying the emotion.

"At Jim... Not you, Shayla," he whispered. "It took everything in me not to kill him, but I can't... Not yet."

I took in his words, sensing there was something behind them that he wasn't saying.

"There is a reason you can't kill him yet, isn't there?"

"Well... A couple," he said, frowning. "If I kill him now... If I kill him here, there will be a lot of questions and it puts you in danger. I promised you freedom. Prison wouldn't give you that."

"What's the other reason?" I asked, taking in his face.

"For me to stay, I collect evil souls for the reapers," he said, shifting. "They want to save this town. For them to do that, the soul must recognize their sins. They must experience guilt. The more tortured a soul is, the better. So, before Jim dies, he will have to feel a lot of pain and fear, but most importantly, guilt."

"And if you don't kill?" I asked, my chest becoming heavy.

"I'll have to leave you," he whispered, his hands brushing my cheeks. "And I promised you I never would. I intend to keep that promise."

My bottom lip trembled as I thought of life without Hunter. I closed my eyes and a tear fell down my cheek because I realized that, no matter what, one day, Hunter would have to leave me in this world alone. I knew that once those who had harmed us were gone, his justice would be over, and any other deaths would darken his soul.

JIM CAME TO MY BEDROOM to remind me again of the story I had to tell, Hunter's anger returned. It took a long while for Hunter to calm down after Jim left. His anger crackled through the room like electricity. He was pacing rapidly in front of me, my eyes following him.

"He's not going to hurt you again," he said, stopping in the middle of the room. "I promise. I will kill him before he does that. Belinda's torture will have to be enough for the reapers."

The light bulb next to me burst, causing me to jump. He glanced at it, his face darkening as he saw my wide eyes.

"I'm sorry, Shayla," he said, closing his eyes. "It kills me that you're frightened of me right now."

I shook my head as he looked at me. "I'm frightened for you... Not of you," I whispered, realizing how dark his temper was already becoming.

He sighed, moving toward me, his expression softening. "How could you be frightened for me?" he said, shrugging. "I'm already dead. They can't hurt me."

"Maybe they can't... But if you continue after they are gone, it can darken your soul. I can already see it happening," I said, swallowing because the next words sent a sharp pain through me. "I would never want that to happen, not even if it means you l—."

He sat on the bed beside me. "Don't say the rest of that sentence," he said, his anger shifting to sorrow. "I'm not leaving you."

I stared into his eyes, my heart breaking. His life had been taken in retaliation because I had wanted my freedom. I wouldn't let his soul die for trying to achieve it again.

"I'm not worth this... I'm not worth that chance," I said, trembling as tears rolled down my cheeks. "I'm not worth losing who you are."

He cupped my cheeks, and it amazed me how much I felt his touch in that moment. His eyes bore into mine. "You are worth everything," he said, his eyes shining with love for me even after all the times I had been used and hurt... Even after my own soul had been dirtied. "I love you, Shayla, which means that I will always put you before myself. Do you understand that?"

"I do because it means the same for me," I said, a tremble rippling through me. "That's what I'm trying to do."

"Then, instead of asking me to leave, be my light when it gets dark," he said, his thumbs caressing my cheeks. "When I get dark, remind me who I am."

I nodded, and his lips touched mine. His love poured into me, and I wondered how I could show him the light when all I had ever known was darkness, but to save him, I would try.

Chapter Nineteen/
Hunter

SANCTUARY... I USED to think of it as a religious word, but as I watched Shayla sleep off another round of pain pills, I realized that *she* was my sanctuary. She gave me refuge and peace and kept me on the right path... Not wanting the darkness to touch me while I enacted justice against the squalid people who hurt her.

I reached forward and touched her, unable to deny myself the pleasure of feeling her skin. It was true that I could feel her more than in life. I didn't lie to her about that, but I wondered if it bothered her not to be able to reach out and touch me. There was a simple pleasure in my fingertips gliding across her skin that was forbidden to her.

I closed my eyes and sighed. She meant so much to me and yet I couldn't give her this simple thing.

"Your soul is melancholy," The reaper's voice cut through the silence.

I jerked, startled by the broken quiet. I turned toward him, unable to hide the deep sadness I experienced because of this thing... In a simple touch, I failed in giving comfort to Shayla.

"A lot has happened tonight," I whispered, the darkness of my thoughts marring my being... My soul.

"And yet, we are pleased with the work you have done," he said, his hood twitching as he tilted his head.

"I don't mean any offense, but your pleasure means little," I said, glancing at Shayla as she slept. "Only her safety has meaning."

He nodded, a ripple of light sparking from him and illuminating the edge of his jaw before it fell back in shadow.

"You love her," he said, simply. "You want to give her more than safety?"

"I want to give her something impossible," I said, my soul aching with the image of what would have been as I wished for life.

The reaper nodded again, that light sparking once more before fading as quickly as it had before. "I know your pain," he said, his voice raspier than before. I wondered for a moment if the reaper was capable of tears. "I once experienced it."

"You were mortal?" I asked, glancing at him skeptically. "You never told me."

"I suppose it's something that haunts me." His cloak twitched again. "It is hard to speak of. However, I believe I could help if you tell me what you assume is impossible."

My eyes moved back to Shayla. "A touch... A simple touch."

The cloak twitched again. "You can touch her."

I nodded. "But she can't touch me, and I wonder—."

"If it bothers her?" The reaper asked, his voice filled with understanding.

Perhaps he had lived through something similar.

"Yes," I said, reaching out to touch her cheek with the tips of my fingers. She moved, causing her face to sink through my hand.

The reaper nodded again, taking a step toward me. "I believe that a gift should be given after your... diligence in justice," he said, his voice creating another light that stayed a little longer before fading.

"A gift?" I asked, frowning.

"A touch," the reaper said, his voice lighter than before. "A place where you can feel her, and she can feel you. A place that is safe for you both."

"That's possible?" I asked, the pain in my soul becoming lighter.

The reaper nodded again. "Did you know the dead can visit dreams?"

"A dream?" I asked, as my eyes widened. "I've heard of the newly deceased visiting dreams. I always assumed it was superstition. Then again, I had assumed that reapers were, too."

"Usually, it is the newly deceased who do, but older spirits have been known to do so as well. The reason why it is possible is that dreams happen in a place between life and death. It's a bridge." the reaper took a step forward. "When the dead visit, the ensuing dreams are vivid. Taste, sight, hearing, and touch are all amplified."

"So, I can enter her dreams and she can touch me?" I asked, my eyes wide with hope.

"Yes," he said, turning toward the door, making me rise to take a step forward.

"Please don't leave," I said, afraid he would leave me with another riddle to solve.

"I'm not," he said, locking the door before turning to a dresser and waving to move it to block the door with the wave of his hand. "I'm simply making sure she is not vulnerable while you visit her."

I relaxed, moving to sit beside Shayla as he turned toward me again. "Now, you simply put one hand on her heart and one on her forehead. The heart will lead you to her, her mind will pull you in."

"Thank you," I whispered, grateful as I reached toward her.

"You're welcome," he said, fading back into the abyss, where he would wait for more souls.

My hands trembled as I neared her skin, hesitating before placing my hands over her heart and forehead. I closed my eyes as my soul reached for hers and I was thrust into the veil between the worlds.

A MYRIAD OF IMAGES flashed through my mind, broken and fractured, as I traveled to Shayla. An image of her mother as she danced in her mother's skirts, her father, his face twisted in anger, Belinda with a belt dripping with water, hitting Shayla, leaving marks against her skin and Jim, his face twisted as he held her down. I wanted to close my eyes against them but couldn't. Finally, I found myself standing in her bedroom.

I frowned; afraid I had been pushed out of her dream until I found Shayla standing in the center of the room. Her blue eyes searching her surroundings as if confused before her gaze landed on me.

"Hunter?" she said, stepping forward, her lips pursing in confusion.

"It's okay, Shayla," I said as she stopped in front of me, mere inches between our bodies.

She blinked. "I thought I was... Somewhere else."

I reached forward and touched her cheek. "You were... In another dream, but I wanted you here with me."

"Another dream?" she asked, her frown deepening. "Are you saying this is a dream?"

I nodded, "A dream but real to us both," I said as I reached forward. She leaned her cheek against my palm.

Her eyes widened as she reached up and touched my hand. "Hunter, I can... I can touch you?"

"Here you can," I whispered, wrapping my arm around her, pulling her against me. We both gasped as our bodies touched, giving way to a myriad of emotions... Excitement, care but most of all, love.

"How?" she asked breathlessly as her fingertips ran over my cheeks, my lips and then settling over my chest. For a moment, I swore my heart jumped, but that wasn't possible. I was dead.

"The reaper taught me how to enter your dreams," I said, a smile moving across my face.

Her hand traveled to my cheek, her fingers fluttering across my skin as tears fell from her eyes. Her lips trembled as I leaned forward, pressing my lips against hers. Her hands moved to tangle in my hair, pulling me closer. My tongue traveled across her lips, and she gasped, allowing me entrance as a tremble swept through her.

She pulled back to stare into my eyes as her face brightened. "Can you do this every time I sleep?"

I nodded, brushing my fingers through her hair. "Every time you dream, I will be here."

"Then I may never want to wake up," she whispered as she rested her cheek against my chest. "I may want to stay here with you forever."

I smiled, pulling her close as I sighed. "Regardless of where you are... Awake or asleep... I will be there with you, but I think we will both look forward to the times you dream the most."

I sighed again, feeling as though there were a heaven after all while sending a silent thank you to the reaper as Shayla's touch moved across my skin.

Chapter Twenty/ Shayla

MY HANDS GLIDED OVER his skin as my heart leaped in my chest and my mouth parted in awe at the sensation of my fingertips against his skin. I had been touched plenty, but his touch, and the ability to touch him, were different... More intimate than anything I had ever experienced. There was nothing dirty or painful about it. It was beautiful and pure... A simple way to show love. One that I didn't even realize I missed because I was content simply being with him.

I trembled as his mouth met mine again, our tongues clashing against each other, his teeth scraping over my bottom lip, as he pulled me flush against him, our chests pressed together and for a moment. Images of what had been done to me infiltrated my mind, turning this precious moment dark and leaving me sullied.

He paused, pulling away from me. "Shayla," he whispered, running his hands through his hair. "I'm sorry. I wasn't thinking... About what you've been through."

I shook my head as I stepped into his arms. I imagined his heart beating in sync with mine even though I knew that to be impossible.

"I want this, but I can't stop my mind from... Remembering," I said, embracing him slowly. "Like this... It's pure. I know you won't hurt me but there is still fear and... Shame."

He nodded. "I understand."

It was a simple statement but one that meant the world to me. "Can we go slower?"

He smiled. "As slow as you want and if you feel you can't go further, we'll stop."

I pressed my lips against his inhaling his spicy scent, allowing all that he was to sink into me. Each touch was slow until our breaths came fast and hard as his fingers dug into my hips, showing me how much I affected him and still, even through the fear, I wanted more... More of him in this world... More of us.

"I love you, Shayla," he whispered against my lips, his voice ripe with emotion. His breaths touched my skin, warming them with his words and branding them deep within my soul.

"I love you too," I said, breathless from his kisses and the way I leaned into him without passing through him. I traced my finger over his cheek and down his jaw before touching it to his lips and moving down his neck to his chest. "I don't want this to end. I can't get enough of being with you this way."

My hands skimmed over his shirt before sliding beneath, gasping when my fingertips met the warm skin of his rippling abdomen. He kissed me again as he backed me toward the bed.

"I want you," he said, his voice strained, pulling me closer as my eyes widened. "I never thought it would be possible... But... Maybe we can try. "

I was unable to speak, unsure of how intimate we could be, but whatever he was able to give me, I would take and whatever pleasure I could offer, I would give. Slowly, I nodded as my heart picked up in speed. It was the first time I had a choice, and my choice would always be him.

His lips crashed into mine before gripping my nightgown, only breaking the kiss to pull it over my head, leaving me naked except for my panties before throwing it to the floor.

His eyes darkened as he took a step back, taking in every inch of my body with a heat I had never witnessed in anyone's eyes before. It was a heat that spoke of affection, not possession and gentleness, without a hint of exhibiting power over me. He bit his bottom lip before reaching for me and laying me gently on the bed.

He pulled his shirt over his head, tossing it to the floor. My eyes widened at his beauty. He was a masterpiece of taut, tanned skin and rippling muscle, and I longed to brush my fingers over each inch of him as I helped him pull the shirt from his body.

He fell on top of me. His hand cupped my cheek as he stared into my eyes, his own gaze softening. "I've never seen anyone so perfect," he whispered and, though I usually would, I wouldn't deny it. The affection and admiration in his eyes told me he spoke the truth.

His lips brushed over mine and down my jaw, tender as the brush of a feather but as potent as a flickering flame across my skin. I arched against him as he showed me his love for me with each kiss and each caress.

He reached for my breast, cupping the weight of one in the palm of his hand before taking a peak in his mouth. I arched as a gasp issued from between my lips, amazed that I sensed every action, every touch. He moved back and blew gently over the taut nipple, causing my core to clench before moving to the other breast to do the same.

He traveled down my body, leaving kisses on my ribs and over my stomach before gripping my panties and pulling them down my legs. He discarded them on the floor. I inhaled sharply as he did the one thing no one had ever done because my body had been a means for their pleasure and not my own. My eyes widened as the intensity of his kisses on my most intimate place arched my back in a spasm of pleasure, a moan escaping from between my lips.

"Hunter," I breathed, gripping his hair as he continued, my body tensing as pleasure washed through me, igniting my nerves. I couldn't tell him this was the first time I had felt that sensation without shame.

I couldn't tell him that it mattered so much because it was with him. I couldn't tell him how much being with him washed away the pain because when I thought of sex, I now would remember this moment and not what had been forced upon me.

He kissed my thighs, moving away from me to take off his jeans. I met his gaze with no anxiety... no pain... no need to hide from him. Instead, I only felt immense love and adoration.

I took in each inch of his body as he exposed it to me, unafraid as he moved toward me, his weight pressing me into the mattress while he gazed into my eyes.

"You have always been the one for me, Shayla," he whispered, his lips moving over my cheeks. "You have always been the one I've wanted...Not only in this way but also in every other way. You are part of me. You are part of my soul."

I ran my fingertips over his jaw. "I have always thought the same of you. I have always been yours, but you've always been mine, too... soul deep," I whispered as he pressed into me. I hooked my legs around his hips as he kissed me and entered me slowly. His body moving with a gentleness I had never experienced.

My hands moved down his back as his pace picked up, causing a pleasurable heat to settle in my stomach, tightening my muscles and traveling to my core. I leaned my head back, clinging to him as I moaned his name.

His lips moved over my neck and, as my body trembled, and I urged him to move faster. I tensed, scoring his back with my nails, coming undone and pulling him over the edge with me. My name came to me as a whisper on his lips. He pressed his forehead against mine, his caresses telling me that this moment had been as important for him as it had for me.

As he rolled beside me and pulled me against him, I didn't ponder over the complexity of our relationship. I didn't think of the fear that existed outside of the dream. I only relished in the fact that, for the first time in my life, I loved someone who loved me in a way too great to explain with words and I knew that no matter what happened, Hunter was the only man I would ever love.

Chapter Twenty-one/
Hunter

SHAYLA AND I LAID NEXT to each other after waking, my hand gently caressing her face. The tenderness of what happened within the dream remained and would remain as long as I existed. I stared into her eyes, my heart warming as I took in her face.

Shayla was the most beautiful girl I had ever known. From the moment I first saw her, I was overwhelmed. As soon as her eyes had met mine on the beach, she had taken a piece of my soul with her, and I had taken a piece of hers. It was a bitter reality that we could have been together long before I died, and I could have helped her while still alive, if only I had known.

I sighed, pushing those thoughts away.

Though I wanted to stay beside her all day, I had a job to finish... One that would free her from her stepmother and, eventually from the man who had harmed her and Desi and who had killed me.

"No matter what you hear below, don't come down," I said softly as her eyes widened. "It will be a few more days before I rid your stepmother from your life."

"As much as I want that, I still worry for your soul," she said, her eyes closing for a moment before opening with tears shining within them. "This death and destruction must be darkening it. I don't understand how it wouldn't."

I shook my head. "It's not darkening it... Not when it's for a reason," I said with a sigh. "I'm not killing to simply kill. I'm not torturing simply to torture. It is punishment. It is justice. It's different from revenge. They aren't innocent, Shayla."

"It's still dark," she whispered and then bit her bottom lip. "Darkness stifles light and I don't want that for you."

"Shayla, you've been through a lot of dark things, but I still see the light in you," I said, staring into her beautiful eyes. "As long as there is light in you, there will be light in me."

She smiled sadly. "I hope that's true."

"It is true," I said, raising my brow. "Don't you want to rid the world of those who have hurt you... Who would hurt others? Don't you want justice?"

She nodded as a tear slid down her face. "You know I do."

"And this town will never give it to you," I said, caressing her cheek, absorbing the tears there. Her worry and love for me seeped into my soul. "This is the only way to do it."

"I understand that," she said, her eyes meeting mine. "But I want to protect you."

I kissed her forehead. "I know, but I will be fine."

She nodded, but I could tell she still wasn't convinced. I caressed her cheek once more.

"Stay here," I said, kissing her before moving through the door. I closed my eyes. Her worry for me was heavy upon my soul as I walked down the stairs.

I FOUND BELINDA WITH salt poured around her. I rolled my eyes as I moved across it. Maybe that would work for other spirits, but not for me. A laugh rumbled through me, bursting from my lips as I leaned close to her ear.

"Did you really think that you could escape me so easily?" I whispered, causing her to jump to her feet. I flicked her hair, now cut in a choppy faux hawk with the tips of my fingers.

"Nice haircut." She moved, stumbling through me. Another sin she had committed played through my mind as she passed.

Shayla stood in the middle of this room. She was around fourteen years old. I saw the girl I had met at the beach within the slightly rounder features of her face, making my soul quake with the love I felt for her as her body trembled.

Belinda ran water over a belt in the kitchen. Shayla's eyes widened, terrified, as she watched her stepmother over the island separating the rooms.

She came toward her with a sick smile on her face, the belt hanging in her hand, dripping water from its ends. The first blow left such a mark that I winced in sympathy, rage building at the woman inflicting Shayla's pain.

"Only fourteen more to go," she said, her voice twisting in a sick way that made my stomach turn. "Happy Birthday."

I moved away from where Belinda was still standing inside my bubble and the vision shattered around me, slicing into my soul.

I glanced around the room and found the belt conveniently hanging from a hook near the kitchen.

Belinda was too terrified to notice what I was doing as I removed the belt from the hook. She continued to glance around the room with eyes so wide they almost took up half of her face.

I ran the water in the sink, soaking the belt thoroughly. Belinda's gaze moved toward the sound of running water, a tremble working through her as she watched the belt float toward her.

"No," she pleaded as I came closer.

"Your sins are there in your mind," I said, narrowing my eyes. "I can see them all. You struck a child intending pain for what reason?"

"She disobeyed," Belinda's voice trembled as she lied. She had clearly wanted to make Shayla hate the day she was born.

"Disobeyed?" I asked, shaking my head. "What type of disobedience would result in such a punishment? None! You simply hated her because she was Ellie's daughter. She was innocent."

"Innocent?" Belinda laughed, but it was mirthless. "She's a whore, sold and bought for sex."

"Sold by you," I growled, lashing out, the belt wrapped around her waist, A blood-curdling scream tore from her throat as she ran toward the door. I gripped her shoulder, throwing her to the ground.

"Did you really think you could run?" I asked, angry that she had tried when Shayla had stayed and accepted a punishment she didn't deserve.

"No matter where you go, I will find you. You will hurt and suffer all that you deserve. And then you will die."

I slung the belt again. This time it wrapped around her shoulder with a smack. The skin just below the short sleeve turned red before welting. Blood rose to the surface and my lip curled.

"Only twelve more," I said through gritted teeth. "But maybe I should give you more."

I swung the belt and Belinda curled in a ball on the floor as I whipped the belt against her again and again. The slap of the belt rang out through the apartment, but her sobs drowned them out.

"P-Please, I can't take anymore!" Belinda cried, her tears almost choking her.

"But a child could?" I asked angrily, slinging the belt again.

I noticed blood seeping through her clothes, and I wondered how many times Shayla had been beaten until her welts burst open. She screamed.

The belt whipped through the air. Belinda's pleas now mumbled through the apartment.

"How many times did Ellie's daughter beg you to stop?" I asked, slinging the belt again as she tried to escape. "How many times did you laugh and continue?"

"Sh-She quit," Belinda sobbed.

"What was that?" I asked, the anger boiling through me.

"Sh-She stopped begging," she said, hiccupping over her tears, clearly hoping the truth would save her. "Sh-She stopped fighting."

I glanced upwards, my heart breaking. I knew why she stopped fighting. She realized there was no way out.

My mind reeled with the weight of Shayla's suffering, and I put as much force as I could behind the belt. The sickening slap of leather upon skin reverberated through the air as it slashed across her back with the force of a whip over and over again.

Belinda tensed, her whole body writhing as her screams echoed through the air. "Know that this won't be the last time," I said, wanting her afraid of my presence like she had made Shayla afraid of hers.

Belinda's sobs continued long after I had stopped, but my heart broke for the woman in the room above me. I wondered how she did not break under the pressure of the life she had been given.

I started to put the belt back where I'd found it but decided that Belinda would hide it if I left it where she could find it. I found a good hiding place where I could retrieve it at will, but it was unlikely that Belinda would, and walked toward the stairs, my soul quaking.

I slipped through the door to find Shayla sitting on the bed with tears falling down her cheeks. What she didn't understand was that the moment her eyes met mine, I found the light that would cure any darkness I suffered.

Chapter Twenty-Two/ Shayla

JUSTICE... THE MEANING of the word is so close to revenge that it is often used as a synonym, but I understood the difference as the familiar sound of leather against skin met my ears, followed by Belinda's screams.

I found no joy or peace in justice because my mother and father still lay dead in their graves. My innocence had still been taken, and I had still borne years of abuse.

Still, the punishment was given, fair in its deliverance, distributed in a way equal to what had been done to me. It didn't bring a smile or lift any of the pain. Instead, it gave only a sense that something righteous had been done... Something that matched the sins of the one receiving the punishment.

The world didn't darken as it would with revenge fueled by hate. Instead, it would lighten because the burden of my suffering in the dark alone disappeared, and the pain received by the abused had been acknowledged.

"You understand now," the raspy voice that entered my room Interrupted my thoughts. It washed over me, sending goosebumps over my skin as I jerked my head up to gaze at the intruder. The sound faded from around me to be replaced with only the breaths coming from me and the cloaked man who stood in the center of my room. His cloak concealed his face in a way that only hinted at the shadows of a face within its darkness. I sensed before I spoke that this being was more than mortal... More than immortal but supernatural, as I took in his tall form hidden behind a black cloak that gave no indication of the shape of his body beneath it. I scrambled backwards on my bed, fear of this creature a reflex more than an emotion.

"Who are you?"

"I know you've been told of me, Shayla," he said, tilting his cloaked head, revealing only the curve of his chin in his hood's shadow. I sensed he studied me as I studied him, but I was sure he was drawing more of a conclusion about who I was than I would ever be able to draw from him.

"The reaper?" I asked, a tremble sliding through me because I realized how quickly my life could end at his hands. Though I wasn't usually afraid of death, I was worried about being separated from Hunter.

"You fear me, but not Hunter?" he asked, his voice hinting at amusement. "You shouldn't fear me. I am not here for your soul, nor do I wish to harm you. You are an innocent."

I frowned, taking in the reaper's rippling robe before trying to find some definition to his face but finding only that curve to his chin draped in shadows. "Then what are you here for?"

He was silent for a long moment before he sighed. "Redemption... And a promise."

"Redemption from what?" I asked, tilting my head as I stared into the shadows hiding his face.

"You don't want to hear about the promise first?" He asked, clearly surprised. I suppose I understood. Most cared only about what they got out of a situation and a promise would appeal to that. I cared little about words that rarely came true.

"Forgive me, but promises usually mean very little to me,"` I said, tilting my head as I relaxed. "Usually, they are broken after they are given."

"Yet, you believe them coming from Hunter," he said, bowing his head slightly.

I narrowed my eyes, ready to defend the man I loved. "Are you saying I shouldn't?"

"Not at all," he said with a sigh. "If anything, you should believe him more than any other."

He was silent for a moment, shifting and causing his robes to ripple around him more.

"I want to explain, but I see I will have to do this your way. The truth is, I am envious that Hunter was allowed to mete out justice for you while you live and breathe because there was a time when I wasn't able to do the same for the one I love."

My heart squeezed at his admission and, though his face remained hidden, and I did not know him, I pitied him. "I'm sorry."

"It's no fault of yours, sweet girl," he said with a sigh that held all the regret of his loved one's death. "But I wondered if I should warn him away from a relationship with you. It is, after all, unnatural, but then, I realized it was often said my relationship with the woman I loved was unnatural too, and that changed my view of things."

I frowned, trying to understand. Maybe he had loved her as a reaper while she was human.

I shook my head. "Unnatural or not, I want to be with him."

"What if the cost is high?" The reaper asked, a sadness in his voice that pierced my heart. "Would you still want him to stay with you?"

"If it's something that hurts him, no," I said, swallowing over the pain of that possibility. "But otherwise, I would want him by my side."

"There is only one thing that could hurt him. You're worried about his soul," he stated, nodding his head. "But you know the difference between justice and revenge. Yes, there is anger with both, but Hunter hasn't stepped over the line. His soul is still as pure as it was in life."

I sighed in relief, not realizing how much I needed to hear that, and I immediately was grateful he had been kind enough to relieve that worry. "Thank you."

"You think my reassurance is my redemption for wanting to warn him away from you," he said softly. "But it's not. My redemption comes in a promise."

"A promise?" I asked, raising my brow because I realized I believed he would keep any oath he uttered.

"You were meant to be together in life, but it was taken away. Hunter was not meant to die," he said, softly. "He was meant to be with you. That's why neither of you will be happy without the other, even in death. So, though, most souls go somewhere else when they pass. I can promise your soul will remain with Hunter. So, during life, you will be with him and upon your death, you will join him. I promise that you both will remain together. That is my redemption for asking him to do this dark work. I only ask that you don't tell him about my visit."

I frowned as suspicion crept into my mind. "Why?"

"He is very protective of you," he said, his voice low. "I sense he would not appreciate my visit as much as you do."

I winced. The reaper was probably right. Hunter would be angry that I was so close to a being that could snuff out my life, especially one he barely trusted. His worry was enough to keep me quiet. After all, the reaper had not made a move to harm me.

"Fine," I said, as his hooded head bobbed.

"Then the promise shall be carried out upon your last breath. The next time you see me will be the moment of your death, but perhaps with this promise, it won't be as terrifying as it sounds," he said, fading from my room.

As he did, Hunter slipped through the door. His eyes met mine and, for the first time since I began to fret about his soul, I could look into his eyes and see the light.

Chapter Twenty-Three/ Hunter

I STEPPED TOWARD SHAYLA as Belinda's sobs echoed through the apartment. Shayla's eyes glistened as she glanced toward the door with her hands clasped in her lap, a frown crossing her face.

"I understand now why your soul won't darken," she whispered, her voice trembling. "Justice isn't something that happens because you enjoy it. It happens for the pain a person has caused. They get back what they have given exactly."

I nodded as I sat beside her on the bed. "I'm glad you understand. I don't do any of it out of joy for their pain but payment for what they've caused. Yes, there is anger but there is a sense of truth behind it all... Exposing their sins for them to see and placing guilt, they can't deny upon their heads," I said, frowning. "It's not something I would ever enjoy doing and I would never knowingly do it to an innocent person. Thankfully, I'm in a position to perceive whether someone is innocent or not.

"I'm thankful for that," she said, glancing at me, her face coloring as she shifted on the bed. "She paid her dues for the wet belt?"

"Not enough," I said, raising my brow as my soul ached for her, knowing it had happened more than once. "This one was for your fourteenth birthday."

She nodded, her eyes darkening with the memory. "That was one of the worst beatings. Jim stopped her from doing it again. It left bruises. I was damaged goods."

I reached forward and touched her arm. The memory of every time she was hit with the wet belt swamped me. Sometimes, she wasn't fully healed from the times before. My whole being pulsed with her pain.

"You see now that it won't fully take away the pain of what has been done to me, but I can experience a sense of righteousness that she now knows exactly what kind of damage she has caused and that she feels the same desperation I did," she whispered.

I nodded, taking in her words, "There's something I need to tell you," I said, frowning because I still hadn't told her about her father's attempt to stop drinking and Belinda's part in his failure to do so.

Keeping it from her didn't seem right, especially now that she spoke of the truth of justice given.

"It sounds bad," she said, her eyes darkening with the worry at what I was going to say, but I wouldn't keep it from her.

"It's about your dad," I whispered, wishing that I could take the pain that would come with what I was about to tell her and knowing I couldn't., I hoped she would experience some peace from knowing that he wanted to stop for her.

"The same day that Jim arrived last," I said, his name causing her to tense. "I was punishing Belinda. When I touched her, I saw one of her sins. Your dad was trying to stop drinking... For you. He loved you, Shayla. He loved you enough to try, but Belinda... She taunted him with a drink and, as an alcoholic—. "

Her eyes swirled with sadness so heart-wrenching that every ounce of light evaporated. "He gave in." The heaviness of those words sank into me.

I nodded. "Belinda gave an excuse. She knew he would leave her if he was sober."

"I-I've always known she was at least partially responsible for his death," she sighed, shaking her head. "Still, I can't put the full weight upon her. He chose to drink in the first place. He chose her and continued to do so over my safety because he wasn't strong enough to stop his addiction. So, though Belinda fed those addictions, he was responsible, too."

"Do you hate him?" I asked, wondering because of her harshness when speaking of him.

She shook her head. "It seems that way, but no. I love him still, but he will never be on a pedestal. The memories of happiness I had of him before my mother's death have faded away under the abuse. So, my love for him is based on the knowledge there was once a good man in him. The things he did to me to appease Belinda were a selfish sacrifice, and that's on him. So, though I love that he could still be a good man if he had lived, I don't like the man he became. After all, his decisions are what led me here. They are ultimately what led you to where you are and what led to Desi being hurt."

I reached forward to caress her cheek. She closed her eyes, relishing my nearness before I frowned. Something was happening because even as I touched her, my hand began to fade from her.

"Shit!" I said, realizing I hadn't pilfered energy in a long while. "I forgot to recharge. Lock the door until I return."

Her eyes widened in fear as she rose from the bed, running to the door, locking it. With the last of my energy, I pushed the dresser against the door once she returned to her bed, hoping it would be enough protection until I returned.

Darkness surrounded me as a thumping sound lulled me into the dark abyss, I was forced into each time my energy drained from me.

THE DARKNESS FADED as the light washed over me from the center of the room. The thumping still sounded in the space surrounding me, becoming quicker in tempo. The reaper appeared in the center of light, his hood twitching as he appeared to tilt his head to the side, taking in the thumping as if it were music.

"Take me back," I said, my voice weak.

"You are out of energy," he said, his voice even, but there seemed to be extra meaning behind each word. "Even my powers don't extend to allow you access back when you need to replenish."

The thumping sped up. "What is that sound?"

"You don't know?" He asked, his voice showing the only hint of emotion I had ever heard from him.

"I wouldn't ask you if I did," I said, frustrated.

"It's her heartbeat," the reaper said, his cloak moving around him.

"Shayla's?" I asked, confused as to why I was able to hear it.

A nod moved the reaper's cloak. "I have only witnessed this once in my long existence," he said, his voice trembling with emotion I didn't realize he could have. "There was once a man who was taken before it was his time... Murdered. He left behind a woman who he loved. They bonded after his death the way they would have bonded in life. Then he would hear her heartbeat. You see... The soul beats the same as the heart, continuing long after death. That is the actual sound you are hearing... Her heart and soul beating for you."

The thumping quickened and my soul trembled. "Why is it so fast?"

"She's frightened," the reaper answered simply. "But her fright will end soon. Your time here runs short. Remember to recharge before going to her. You don't need this to happen again."

I wanted to ask more about the man he mentioned. I wanted to know what became of the couple, but the light pulled me away and I found myself on the street outside Shayla's home. I pulled the energy from seven cars and turned to Shayla's apartment, moving toward her, wanting to take away every bit of fear from her life.

Chapter Twenty-Four/
Shayla

I WATCHED HIM FADE away from me, and though he said he would be back, the sheer terror of the possibility that he wouldn't be able to return paralyzed me.

I trembled as I glanced around, truly alone for the first time since he had become my protector... My love. My bottom lip trembled as I closed my eyes, remembering every word that the reaper had said, landing like toxic kisses on my mind.

The reaper had offered me a way to be with him forever and even as I tried to push it away; the thought remained... Death... Peace... A way to be with Hunter when I couldn't really be with him here. A way to be happy with him forever.

I swallowed, pushing the thoughts away. No matter how strong my desire, I understood that Hunter would be upset if I gave up my life when all he wanted to do was breathe again... Have a heartbeat... Tell his parents and sister he loved them, and embrace them. To him, life was precious and if I gave it up it would be a sin.

I took a deep breath, almost convincing myself to calm down until my phone dinged a text notification. I stared at it as if it was a bomb, and it was. The only person who sent me texts was Jim, and it was only for one reason.

I moved toward it, my hands shaking as I picked it up. I had one week before I was sold again... One week before, my hellish life became worse than it already was. Without Hunter, I had no ally against it. Without Hunter, I had nothing. He was my everything.

A tear fell down my cheek as I crumpled to the floor, hugging my knees to my chest, fighting the fear of what was to come. After Hunter had given me so much hope, the despair of not knowing that Hunter would return, and the prospect of returning to that life left me drowning in despair... And even if he could return, how would he be able to protect me when there were so many monsters to protect me from? How could I protect myself if he didn't return when there was only one way out? I just laid there, curled in a ball on the floor, crying out all my fears and praying for escape.

The phone's notification sounded again. Jim's name popped across the screen, causing the weight on my chest to become heavier. A sob broke from me as I hoped for relief but it was hard to find it when I was trapped in the darkness.

"SHAYLA," HUNTER'S VOICE washed over me and for a moment, I wondered if I imagined it. "I'm here."

I raised my head to peer into his beautiful eyes as a sob broke from my throat. Relief and love washed over me as the tears continued to come.

"I-I th-thought you were gone," I said, trembling with relief as the rest of the panic spilled from me. "I-I didn't know if you could come back."

The coolness that I associated with his touch calmed me as he brushed his fingers over my cheek.

"I'm so sorry," he whispered, his eyes darkening in pain as he sat beside me on the floor to rain kisses across my face. "It's my fault. I forgot to pull energy. I won't do it again, Shayla. I promise."

I trembled as I tried to push away the thoughts, but they came anyway. His eyes narrowed as a tear fell through his finger. There was no anger in his gaze, only worry and fear so potent it struck me in the chest.

"Shayla," he whispered, hesitating before he spoke, "Please... Don't ever give up your life... Even if I'm not here. Keep fighting."

I trembled as I moved my phone, so he was able to view Jim's message. "How am I supposed to when the monsters keep coming?" I asked, my bottom lip trembling. "You can't kill them all."

"You're wrong about that," he said, his jaw set in determination.

"I'm not wrong," I whispered, my heart aching. "One day, one of those monsters will get to me. One day, they will hurt me worse than they already have. My life will end."

He shook his head, pain sliding over his face, breaking my heart further. "You don't trust me?"

"I do, but it's too much," I whispered, my lips moving over words that had the power to hurt us both. "There are too many. You can't get justice from all of them, and be with me every second of the day. It's impossible, I don't expect that from you."

He ran his hand through his dark hair. "I'll figure it out," he said, his words shaking from him with so much emotion my heart squeezed, making me want to protect him from the truth, but to do that, I would have to lie.

He closed his eyes, taking a deep breath. "How many men have bid on you?"

Shame slid through me as I contemplated the number of men who had harmed me. "Over a hundred, and it's growing every day."

He winced as if I had slapped him, but his gaze met mine.

"Shayla, this isn't on you. This is not something that is your fault. The shame should be on those men."

"I understand that, but it's still there," I whispered, shaking. "They ruined me. All of them did."

"You're not ruined, Shayla," he whispered, caressing my cheek again. "You are perfect no matter what they've done. One day, I will make you see that. I will wipe those memories away."

I stared at him with words trapped in my throat. How did I tell him what he expected to do was impossible? I would always view myself as tainted goods. I would always notice my imperfections... Even the ones that I didn't cause myself. They would always be there in the recesses of my mind, reminding me that I had been used and abused; that I had been treated as if I were only there for another's pleasure and nothing else. Otherwise, I was meant to be harmed and punished for those things in life I had no control over. I was used as a release for lust, pain, anger, and revenge.

"Shayla," his voice was fading, breaking my heart even more because I was hurting him, and I never wanted to hurt him again. "You are precious. You are the reason why my soul still has light. So, as ruined as you assume you are, you are my salvation from the darkness. You are the reason why I don't step from justice into revenge... Not just for you, but for Desi, too. It would be so easy to cross over into that dark space because I am full of rage at the hurt they caused to you and to her. I want to hurt them worse than they deserve. I want to destroy them where even their souls are no longer in existence, but I won't. I will enact their exact punishments because I know that you don't want me destroyed by the shadows of that anger. So, no matter how ruined you think you are, remember I see you... I see your worth. Your life is more precious than every treasure in this world to me. I will fight to make you see it. I will work for what you assume is impossible. I will find a way to save you from every evil thing that can or will touch you. You must have faith in me. You must trust me. You can't give up."

My bottom lip trembled, knowing he meant every word. "I have faith in you."

He kissed me and though I wasn't lying, I still felt despair because I felt as if I was setting him up for failure. I knew the odds were against me in this life and, even though I wanted to believe he would succeed in protecting me, I couldn't imagine a scenario where he would.

Chapter Twenty-Five/
Hunter

BETRAYAL... IT ECHOED through my mind as soon as I touched Shayla, as she broke apart in front of me. Anger pierced me as I witnessed the discussion between her and the reaper and, though she had promised to keep it secret, I didn't view her as the betrayer because I would have done exactly the same thing in her place. I would have latched on to that one chance of us being together.

My soul trembled as I realized that during my absence she may have perished while I recharged, tempted by the promise that death would bring her. A part of me wondered if that was exactly what the reaper was trying to accomplish.

Shayla laid upon her bed now, calmer while I was with her. Love for her enveloped me as I brushed the hair from her face, determined to show her that she was able to be free while she lived... Determined to show her that her life was worth living. I wondered how I would prove to someone who had been abused by a person from every facet of her life that her ability to breathe, to have a beating heart, was precious.

"Do you know who the winning bidder is?" I asked, glancing at her phone as the words seem to pulse the threat of danger at her, hurting her with each word.

She swallowed, her fear and shame palpable. "This is a special case... One of Jim's special people. He didn't bid. He simply put in a request with the amount of money he would pay. I don't know their names most of the time," she whispered hoarsely. "But this one... I know who he is."

"You've seen him while... Living his regular life?" I asked, frowning as her body trembled beneath my hand.

She nodded, her eyes rimmed red. "I've seen him at his job."

A tear fell down her cheek as she hesitated. "Shayla, tell me," I whispered, caressing her face, wondering why this man was different from the others.

"He's a teacher," she said, her bottom lip trembling. "I had the displeasure of realizing that when assigned to his science class at fourteen."

I frowned as my soul churned with shock and anger.

"What's his name?" I asked through a growl, determined to erase him from her life.

Her eyes met mine, darkness swirling within her blue irises, creating a window to the destruction that constantly tore at her soul. Her bottom lip trembled.

"Luke Richards," she choked over her sorrow, tears filling her eyes because she knew I would recognize the name.

I closed my eyes as the memory of Desi coming home with a piece of paper saying she had been transferred from his class to another due to high test scores entered my mind.

"You got Desi out of his class," I whispered, my soul shaking because I had once punished her for Desi's pain when she only ever wished to protect her.

I opened my eyes, taking in her face, pale with shame, because I understood she had to do some unspeakable things to save Desi, but I refused to make her relive those memories by asking her what she had done.

"I-I couldn't let her be ruined like me," she said, her voice trembling. "I-I guess I failed in the end."

I shook my head. "She's not ruined, Shayla," I said, my soul heavy with her pain. "And neither are you. They are ruined... Their hearts are black, and the thing once known as their souls were replaced with nothing but darkness. You and Desi still have light. I see that in the way you protected her. I saw that in the way she worried I hated her the last night I was with her. I see the capability of love in both of you."

Tears fell down her cheeks as she took a shaky breath. "You're the one with light."

"Then, let me guide you," I whispered, so afraid I wouldn't be able to save her. "Let me show you how things will be better."

She nodded, but I saw her hope waning. Still, if I could show her justice, freedom, and love, perhaps that would be enough.

I fought my rage because as mad as the betrayal made me, I wanted to resist doing the reaper's bidding. I would, though, because it was the only way to lead Shayla to the light. It was the only way I could stay with her, and for her to want to live. For Shayla, the reaper would get another soul.

DOUBLE LIVES... THAT'S what every one of Shayla's abusers had... A double life. Luke Richards was an expert at it. He taught at the elementary school during the day... Respected and loved by his peers.

His wife had died young, and he had never remarried, claiming he would only ever love her. Even his appearance was deceiving. Tall with dark hair... Most women would think he was a handsome man in his early forties. His blue eyes were framed in glasses, giving him an intelligent appearance, and the suits he wore were pressed and well-made, giving him an air of dignity. It surprised me that no one asked where he had gotten the money for such suits. The only logical explanation was that he handed Jim information on the children he taught.

However, I was focused on his residence. He lived alone on the outskirts of town. His nearest neighbor was a mile away and if I wanted to prevent him from harming Shayla, I had to visit him before his scheduled time with her.

Shayla glanced up from her phone, her eyes shining in fear. "You'll have to leave me for a while, won't you?"

I caressed her cheek, hoping what I would say could give her comfort. "I have something to tell you," I whispered softly. "It's something I learned while I was away."

"What is it?" She asked, frowning, fearing the bad... Always fearing the bad.

"We're bonded," I said, staring into her eyes, "So much so that while I was away, I could hear your heart. I'm sure I'll hear it any time I am away from you now."

"So, you'll understand if I'm frightened," she said, frowning, "And maybe if I'm in trouble."

I nodded, "But you won't be in trouble," I whispered, "Because I won't be gone long and you are going to stay locked in your room."

"But Belinda—."

"Is too sore to climb those stairs," I said, reassuring her.

She took a deep breath. "Okay," she said, trying to control her shaking.

I caressed her cheek. "Trust me," I whispered, softly, "When I get back, you'll sleep, and I'll meet you in your dreams. Just stay safe for me until I return. Promise me."

Her eyes darkened, but then she nodded. "I promise."

I kissed her and then faded to search out Luke Richards. The precious sound of Shayla's heartbeat steadily thrummed around me.

LUKE RICHARDS' HOME was a clean, white, two-story residence with a neat yard. The porch leading up to his front door was huge and decorated with a swing. It was yet another thing Luke Richards used to cover the evils he had done in life.

I slipped into the house, surprised to find outdated furniture in the living room. It didn't match his outward persona, with his tailored suits. His wife probably bought them before her death and he had never bothered to update them. Pictures lined the walls, showcasing a couple. Luke Richards was giving the camera a wide smile. His blonde-haired, blue-eyed wife leaned her lithe frame against him. For a moment, I wondered if she realized what kind of man she had married, then shook my head. He was so skilled at wearing a mask, she probably never had.

I tilted my head, hearing a tinkling sound from below, and frowned as I followed it. It led me to a heavy wooden door in the kitchen that seemed as if it was barely used. I found stairs leading down into a cellar with two more doors.

The first cellar room sent a thrill of fear through me. Shackles hung from the walls. The side of the room held a dirty but well-used mattress. I glanced around the room, searching for the source of the sound, but found no inhabitants, and I didn't know whether to be relieved or terrified. I shook my head and peeked through the other door. Three walls were lined in shelves filled with chemicals, but it was the third wall that caused my soul to pulse with nauseating worry and fear...And disgust.

Cork Boards filled with pictures of young girls in various positions of distress assaulted my vision. Each image depicted unspeakable tortures . I didn't need to touch Luke Richards to understand the level of pain he had put them through. and I didn't need to touch him, to realize that these girls were no longer alive. He wouldn't risk them telling his secrets.

A sound came from behind a door across the room. I turned to find Luke Richards, rolling up his white shirt sleeves. A table of sharp knives and syringes and vials filled with different liquids were displayed across the table.

My nostrils flared. The need to give him the same pain he had enacted on Shayla... On these little girls, too intense to let it go.

I eyed the chemicals on the wall, formulating a plan, as I made my way over to his side of the room.

"Luke Richards," I said. He jerked his head up in my direction, eyes darting around me.

"Who's there?" He asked, his eyes holding the hope that he was hearing things.

"Justice," I hissed as he glanced around the room, searching but not finding me. "Karma, kismet or, in your case, doom."

"Where are you?" he asked, a tremble shaking through him as he tried to keep control of himself.

"Everywhere," I said, projecting my voice around him as he backed toward the table. I could tell he was about to piss his pants.

His eyes darted around the room, searching. I smiled, lifting one of the chains and clasping it around his wrist. He gave up control of his bladder as he realized he was trapped, but still couldn't see how it had happened.

"What the hell?" he asked, his voice slurring with fear.

"Hell is exactly what it is," I said, sauntering to his shelves as he struggled. "Except usually it's someone else's hell here and you're the devil. Now, you'll understand exactly what they went through. Now, you'll understand exactly what it feels like to have a devil of your own."

My eyes landed on a shelf, my eyebrows raising as I read the labels... Citric acid... Sulfuric acid... Fluoroantimonic acid... I picked up the last one. I swirled the contents in the Teflon lined bottle, wondering what it could do.

Luke's voice trembled. "No," he said in a whisper as I moved closer to him. He began to pull at the binds, tears building in his eyes.

"No!"

"I'm assuming you used this on those little girls," I said, wondering what kind of pain it gave them as I opened the container, stepping closer to him as he doubled his efforts, trying to pull at his binds. Sweat dampened his dark hair and slid down his face as I reached him.

The contents were clear, the smell strong enough to cause Luke to gasp. I poured some of the foul liquid down his pants leg. His scream rent the air as the acid burned through his leg, making him drop to the ground as the flesh melted away and the bone lost its integrity, gasping for breath as the acid still continued to burn.

The nauseating knowledge that he did this to a child broke through me and I realized no matter what I did to him in this life, it would never be enough.

"Justice is equal punishment, but you've done so much that the afterlife will have to take care of the rest," I said, tipping the container, aiming it for the very thing he used to harm Shayla and countless other girls. Though he was gasping, his scream ripped through the air, crying out for forgiveness, taking the last bit of oxygen from his lungs as I dropped the container beside him and turned. His voice died leaving only the hiss of the acid traveling up his body and through his abdomen before I moved through the door as his soul was released for the reaper. It found me, sifting through me as I walked through his house.

Shayla's heartbeat still echoed around me as I walked down the street and through the night back to the woman I had only begun to avenge, satisfied with the knowledge that I had not only saved her but countless other girls he would have abused and killed. Luke Richards would never be anyone's source of pain ever again.

Chapter Twenty-six/
Shayla

PEOPLE SAY A PROMISE is made to be broken and even knowing that I made one to Hunter I couldn't help but be enticed by the peace death offered me. Of course, death is usually to be feared, but I would look it in the eyes with a smile because it would bring the ability to be with Hunter forever. Yet, there it was... The promise... A promise not to die... A promise to live. Regardless of how torturous my life was, I would fight not to break it.

"Shayla," my head snapped up as Hunter returned. His eyes were dark with the deed he had just done. "He won't touch you... Or anyone else again."

I swallowed because, though justice should give me relief, it only caused a bitter taste in my mouth that would fade as I realized one less person would hurt me. Still, there was a fear that someone new would replace him... Someone worse.

Hunter touched my cheek, temporarily erasing the fear, but there was a darkness in his eyes that hadn't been there before. I frowned, taking in his face, afraid that whatever happened would haunt him.

"What's wrong?" I asked, tilting my head.

"He was much worse than you thought," he said, his eyes dark with pain. "He was a child murderer. There were pictures of his victims plastered across a basement wall. You probably saved Desi from him."

"Oh God," I said as my stomach churned. This man had touched me. He had—.

I ran toward the bathroom, heaving and barely making it to the toilet as I vomited until my stomach was dry. My still healing body ached as I trembled, my hands shook as I wiped my mouth.

"I'm sorry," Hunter said, running his hand through his hair.

I shook my head as I rose to walk to the sink on trembling legs. "Why are you sorry?" I asked, my voice weak and hoarse. "You didn't do this. He did this. If anything, you've prevented the pain of another child."

"I just wish I could have prevented yours," he said, moving his hand over my hair.

I picked up my toothbrush and put toothpaste on it before glancing at him in the mirror.

"You do prevent my pain," I said, taking a deep breath. "You keep those who have hurt me from hurting me again. You keep them from harming other people."

"I guess I just realized that sometimes what they've done in life will never be given justice while they breathe," he whispered, the pain on his face pulsing through the space between us.

"Then, we have to hope that whatever comes after their deaths will offer the justice that they deserve," I whispered, knowing that my words wouldn't ease his torture because words never eased mine.

I CLOSED MY EYES, TUMBLING into my dreams with the anticipation of being able to touch Hunter... To feel him. Sunlight played across my face, causing me to open my eyes. The salty breeze of the ocean kissed my skin as I took in the curving blanket of ocean waves crashing onto the crystalline surface. An immense expanse of the brightest blue stretched across the horizon, with wispy white clouds moving across the surface.

"I thought this would be nice," Hunter whispered softly, his voice losing all the pain from before. "I don't get to go outside much, and you haven't been outside in what probably seems like forever."

It was such a sweet gesture that my eyes welled with tears. He reached forward and caressed my cheek. And that's when I saw them. A very familiar girl and boy chasing each other around the bottom of a pier.

As we stepped closer, I watched as he grabbed her arm and she flinched away and then, he gave her...Me the sweetest kiss. I glanced up at Hunter as tears rested in my eyes as the memory replayed before us. He cupped my cheek, his blue eyes gentle in the summer sun of the most perfect day of my past.

"You're crying," he said, caressing my cheek with his thumb. "You know the rules."

I smiled. "Even for happy tears?"

His lips touched mine. "Especially for happy tears," he said before he kissed me, echoing the sweetness of the past and erasing the sadness of the present for a little while.

AN IMMEASURABLE AMOUNT of time passed as we sat on the beach watching the sun sink below the horizon. The people faded, and it was just the two of us sitting next to each other with my head on Hunter's shoulder, taking in the view before us as the sound of crashing waves lulled me into a sense of peace I hadn't experienced in years.

"This was a perfect dream," I whispered with a sigh, lifting my head to peer at him.

Hunter smiled, his eyes sparkling in the fading sun as the sky lit with blues, pinks, oranges, and purples.

"If I had met you again in life, we would have done this for real," he said, a sigh breaking from between his lips. "But this... This is perfect because nothing from life can harm us here... Nothing dark or ugly can destroy it."

I glanced at the horizon, taking in the now dark sky, sparkling with stars when I realized he was wrong, because the sound of my phone ringing was shattering the dream.

I glanced up at Hunter, tears burning my eyes before I glanced toward the ocean. The darkest thought moved through my mind as I realized this was where I had met him, but it was also his burial place. Jim and his men had buried him in the water where no one would ever find him.

"Shayla," Hunter's voice was far away now. I glanced around the beach, realizing I was alone in the dark.

"Hunter!" I screamed in panic as I turned, trying to find him as the world became a blur. Tears broke my vision as I closed my eyes, squeezing them tight as I tried to remember that this was a dream. There was nothing to be afraid of.

I felt someone shake me, their hands like vices on my shoulders, their desperation to pull me into reality sinking through the dream.

My eyes burst open in the darkness of my room. The phone's notification dinging over and over again. I reached for it on the bedside table as I glanced up to find Hunter. A frown darkened his brow as I answered the phone.

"Shayla," Jim's voice echoed over the line, and I winced. "What took you so long?"

I swallowed, trying to push away the terror of hearing his voice, but still that ever-present fear shuddered through me. "The medicine for my injuries makes me drowsy."

Jim grunted in acceptance of my excuse. "Something fell through with the bidder," he said, his voice sharp with anger.

"Fell through?" I asked, hoping my voice didn't betray that I already knew that the teacher was dead.

"Yes, but don't worry about that," he said, as if trying to reassure me when it was only a promise of more torture. "Instead, another bidder will take his place."

I swallowed as tears burned my eyes. "Another bidder?" I asked as Hunter's gaze snapped toward me, his eyes narrowing.

"Just be ready by Saturday," he snapped. I flinched as my heart dropped.

"I will be," I whispered as he hung up.

Hunter shook his head. "Another bidder?" he asked, anger coloring his voice.

I lowered my head as I tried to control my shaking. Hunter's eyes moved toward me before he sat on the bed next to me.

"Don't worry, Shayla," he whispered, his voice firm in determination. "I'll take care of him, too."

I nodded, but I knew that all hope was lost because even if he killed this bidder, another would take his place. It would be a never-ending stream of abusers that he would be fighting against for the rest of my life.

Chapter Twenty-Seven/
Hunter

SECRETS... EVERYONE had them. Jim was a respected official who shook hands and kissed babies, but behind closed doors, he was a murderer and sexual predator. The men who worked for him were just as dirty, but I was sure they also had separate lives that didn't reflect their sins in the dark. I was equally sure the bidders were the same.

They had forced Shayla to live that double life and her secrets were weighing her down. I sensed them breaking her, and I feared no amount of justice would glue her broken heart and soul back together.

Her phone notification chimed through the room, and she jumped. She stared at the phone with a wariness that terrified me. All I wanted was to save her, but I saw her drowning in the darkness, searching for peace. She picked up the phone with trembling hands, her brow furrowing as she read the message, a sigh breaking from her lips as sorrow twisted through her, settling in her eyes.

"There's another bidder," she said, her voice wary and broken, but there was also acceptance in it and that worried me more than anything else. She was giving up. I sensed it in my soul.

"Did he say who it was this time?" I asked, but she shook her head, her hair curtaining her face.

"He's being overly cautious," she said, her bottom lip trembling. "But I think Belinda would know."

I narrowed my eyes. Belinda had gone long enough without punishment, but I was afraid to leave Shayla. She raised her head and forced a smile that didn't reach her eyes.

"I'm okay," she said and then closed her eyes, taking a deep breath. When she opened them, I almost believed her, but she was so used to wearing that mask preventing the world from seeing her true feelings I knew she was lying. Shayla wasn't okay at all.

"Shayla…"

"I've been through all of this before, damn it!" She snapped and then took a deep breath. "You act like this is something new, but it's not Hunter. This is how I've lived my life for seven years. So, stop acting like I'm fragile."

Her words sank through me like acid, hurting even though I realized they were born from stress and frustration.

"You have to trust me," I said, reaching for her, relieved when she allowed me to brush my fingertips over her skin.

"I do trust you," she said, her words breaking and cutting through me. "But this is too much. There are too many. You can't protect me from them all."

"Then, I'll take out Jim," I said, my soul trembling with a warning in her words, "I'll cut off the head of the snake."

"There are many snakes and many heads," she said softly.

"Someone will take his place. There will always be someone to take his place."

"Then I'll keep killing them until the other snakes are afraid to take that step," I said, determination sliding through me. "But first, let me talk with Belinda. Perhaps I can find out who this new bidder is. I won't have him coming for you while I'm taking care of Jim."

"Okay," she whispered, her eyes downcast.

"I will be right downstairs," I said, caressing her cheek, thankful that I didn't witness any intentions to harm herself in her mind. "I'll be able to hear your heartbeat while there."

She nodded, and I kissed her forehead before leaving the room because if I stayed any longer, I feared I would never leave. If I stayed, she would only fall deeper into the melancholy I was afraid would take her life. Instead, I had to help her the only way I could, and maybe one day she would rediscover the hope that was quickly fading from her eyes.

IT DIDN'T SURPRISE me when I found Belinda on the couch, a bottle of wine gripped in her hand, moving toward her lips. I narrowed my eyes as I took in this woman who had caused so much pain in Shayla's life. Again, I was struck with the thought that whatever I did to her would never be enough.

I reached forward seeing another sin. She was fixing food, humming to herself as she put something from a small white bottle in the gravy before serving it to Shayla, becoming almost gleeful when she became sick. I narrowed my eyes at the bottle she was drinking from.

"Hello, Belinda," I said, causing her to pause with the bottle midway to her lips. "Are you sure that's good to drink? I mean... After all, I could have added something to it."

Her eyes widened as she threw the bottle away from her, her lips quivering. I watched as the wine spilled on the carpet, staining it from a light beige to a deep red.

"Pity," I said with an exaggerated sigh. "You just wasted a perfectly good bottle of wine."

Tears rested in her eyes. "Why did you do that?"

I gave a mirthless laugh. "Really?" I asked, as her hands shook. "I told you I see your sins. Making someone afraid to eat is especially cruel. I thought you deserved to understand what it felt like."

"What else are you going to do to me?" she asked, her voice trembling over the words. "When will it stop?"

I stepped forward. "It won't stop until you're dead and you won't die until I say it's time."

A whimper moved from her lips. "Please."

"Please? Hmmm... I may be feeling generous today," I said, softly. "May, but only if you give me the name of someone, I can enact the same sense of justice on as I have with you."

"Wh-who?" she asked, her breaths moving quickly from her lips.

"Someone who wishes to defile Ellie's daughter even more than she already is. There is a man who bid on Shayla. I want his name," I said, raising my brow.

She hesitated. "You killed the teacher," she said, swallowing.

"I did," I said with a shrug. "But you knew that... Somewhere deep down in that blackened heart and soul... You knew."

"Why would I give you another's name?" She asked, her body rigid.

"Because you care more about yourself more than anyone else," I said, causing her to flinch. "You want a reprieve, don't you?"

She clamped her lips shut. But I understood it had nothing to do with loyalty. She was hoping to get an upper hand when there was not one to be had.

"Just remember, I gave you a chance," I said, moving toward the place where I hid the belt and lifted it so she was able to see what I intended to do. She fell from the couch, moving away from me as I stepped closer.

"P-Please," she said, tears falling down her face.

"Please? Are you begging?" I asked, glancing at the belt. "I haven't even drenched it yet."

Tears rolled down her face. "The lawyer," she said, her voice trembling.

"His real name," I said, stopping a foot from her, dangling the belt in front of her face.

"Aaron Cleaveston," she whimpered, her body shaking so much her teeth chattered.

"Okay," I said, backing away with the belt. "You've earned your reprieve."

She rose to shaky feet. I glanced over my shoulder as she went to the refrigerator, taking out another bottle of wine. She hesitated before drinking.

"Don't worry," I said, rolling my eyes. "It's not poisoned."

She sighed in relief as she took a gulp. Her addiction was obviously giving her pain.

"Of course, I could be lying," I said as a sob broke from her lips. I shrugged, moving up the stairs to Shayla, hoping I could give her some hope before her life drowned her in the darkness.

Chapter Twenty-Eight/
Shayla

I STARED INTO THE MIRROR, my skin paler than usual, as Hunter watched me warily. The cursed determination was written clearly on his face, but I realized no matter what he did, he would fail. He couldn't fight all my demons.

"I love you, Shayla," he whispered, and I knew he did. He loved me as much as I loved him... That was the only reason I tried to live when all I wanted was the peace of death.

"I love you too," I said, turning to take in his face and I saw it there... The panic. Guilt swirled through me as he studied my face, searching for a sign that I was better and knowing he wouldn't find it there.

It felt as if I were in the middle of a lake in the dark, struggling to stay afloat, all the while knowing that it wouldn't end once I reached the shore because there were still demons within the shadows waiting to attack. Yet, still, I struggled... I struggled for him. The problem remained that, even with him there, the demons would attack and though he would fight them, there would be more and more and eventually, he would fail. I didn't know what would happen then. I felt weak... So weak.

I took a deep breath, closing my eyes as his lips touched mine. It was a sweet gesture, but also toxic because I wanted more. I wanted to be with him, to touch him. The promise of the reaper hung in the space between us like a beacon to give me everything I wanted with him and peace... That tempting peace that brought bad thoughts unbidden to my mind.

"I'll have to leave soon if I'm going to take care of the lawyer before tomorrow night," he whispered, his brow furrowing.

"I know," I said, my heart aching with his absence already and with that normal ache came the fear because I would be left unprotected. God, I was weak.

"After this, I'll begin to take out Jim and Belinda," he said, his voice trembling slightly, but I realized it wasn't fear of killing them... It was a fear that I wouldn't survive until then.

I nodded, but he grasped my chin, beckoning me to gaze into his eyes. "Shayla, I will protect you," he said, his voice quivering. "Please, trust me."

"I do trust you, Hunter," I said, speaking the truth. He would do everything in his power to protect me. It was simply the odds were too great.

He nodded; his eyes dark as they moved over my face. "I'll return as soon as I'm done," he said, giving me a smile with so much sadness my heart ached.

I nodded once, watching him go, counting down the seconds until he returned.

THE DOOR OPENED, AND I mentally slapped myself for forgetting to lock it as Belinda limped into the room. Her eyes were rimmed in red as she gazed at me with despair and hate mixed like poison within her eyes.

"There has been a change in plans," she slurred, her words blending as a tremor shook through her.

"What do you mean?" I asked, fear sliding down my spine as I took in her face. It was obvious that the justice she was receiving was destroying her little by little.

"The lawyer," she said, causing my heart to trip over itself. "He's on his way."

"But I'm not supposed to see the bidder until tomorrow," I said, panic settling in my chest. Hunter was gone, but I still couldn't allow him to touch me. I wouldn't. I could only hope that Hunter would hear my heartbeat speeding up and realize that something was wrong enough to return.

Tears settled in my eyes as I glanced around the room with my lip trembling. I hugged my arms across my body.

Belinda narrowed her eyes. "There's no use in crying. It's not like you haven't whored yourself out before."

I flinched at her blunt words. The harshness of them proved she hadn't changed. She would continue to dole out abuse until the day she died.

I raised my chin. "You're right," I said as I straightened. "I should take a shower."

Belinda nodded as she gave a drunken chuckle. "You wouldn't want to stink for the bidder. They may realize you aren't as special as you think you are."

I turned to her, my eyes wide, as anger slid through me. My stomach twisted as she curled her lip as if I was something disgusting. "You think this makes me feel special?"

"Don't you?" Her words slurred as my stomach spun in revulsion, "All these men want you. They are willing to pay for you and risk prison doing so."

"They pay you to force themselves on me," I said, swallowing over the bile rising in my throat. "That doesn't make me special. It makes me something they use and throw away."

She stepped close to me, her rancid breath flowing over my face. "Then it's good you've learned your place. Go take your shower. Your next John will arrive soon, and you better make him happy. If not, you'll deal with me and then, Jim."

Then she turned to stumble out the door. Hot tears fell down my cheeks as I rushed to lock her away from me. I turned, glancing around my room in a panic, looking for a way out but finding none. Hunter had yet to return, though my heart was beating like a drum in my chest.

I dragged myself to the bathroom. My hands shook as I searched it for a way out... A way to prevent this from happening.

"No, please," I whispered to myself, desperation clear as the plea landed in the empty space of the bathroom.

My eyes fell on the mirror as I reached forward, pulling open the medicine cabinet. My eyes fell on the sleeping pills, which whispered its dark promises to me. Peace... Happiness...

My promise to Hunter fell to pieces in my mind as I reached for the pills, the smooth surface of the plastic bottle moving across my fingertips.

I opened the bottle, finding it full. Tears fell down my cheeks, hot and scalding, as I poured them on the bathroom counter. Panic turned to guilt and sorrow as I picked up the first pill.

My breath shuddered from me. "I'm sorry," I said, hoping Hunter would hear it somehow as tears fell down my cheeks, hating myself even more for the promise I was about to break. "I'm so sorry, Hunter."

I picked up five of the pills and put them in my mouth, holding them there, knowing I was standing on the edge of a cliff, posed to jump, and realizing I was going to take that leap. I closed my eyes and swallowed before taking more.

The minutes passed as my heart drummed slower and slower. Drowsiness hit me as I sank to the floor, hoping that Hunter would forgive me. I would find out when I finally passed through that veil. I closed my eyes with his face in my mind, finally reaching for the peace death would bring...the peace I had never gotten in life.

Chapter Twenty-nine/ Hunter

AARON CLEAVESTON WORE his mask well. He was even better at it than the teacher had been. He was handsome with a pretty wife, and a little girl, a respected lawyer who often did pro-bono for the poor. He volunteered at the soup kitchen, helping feed the homeless, and was a member of many of the charities in town. No one would have suspected his sins because that mask made him seem angelic.

Upon arriving at his house, I realized his wife knew nothing of her husband's activities as she hummed in the kitchen. I peered at his little girl, realizing she had no idea of his darkness either. I was relieved he hadn't touched her, though I wondered if that was to keep up the charade. Still, all she saw was her daddy, and I was thankful that at least her life wouldn't be marred by his darkness.

As I glanced at the family pictures, taking in his jovial face, I tried to wrap my head around such a double life. I didn't understand how these men kept up the act without anyone suspecting what they really were. When Aaron Cleaveston died, his wife and daughter would grieve him, probably never knowing what type of man he really was, and I was sure others would too, but he didn't deserve their grief. He deserved their ire.

The man clearly wasn't home. I headed toward his office tilting my head to tune into the steady drum of Shayla's heart, relieved its thump echoed through my ears. I decided to focus on her heartbeat instead of my surroundings. It made the task ahead seem less horrible.

I made my way out of his home, finding his office in the center of downtown in the business district. The building itself appeared as pristine as he did, but I realized more than most that appearances were deceiving, and I wondered if any of his sins stretched to the office before me.

I scanned the front entrance, finding him there. My eyes narrowed on him as he entered the building and I stepped toward it, intending to go after him, but a man stepped in front of me, blocking my way. There was something about the man that kept me from moving past him.

"Hunter," he said, startling me. I studied him, searching for a reason why he sensed me near. He was a muscled man with skin darker than mahogany. His light brown eyes bore into me as he stared into my face, unnerving me as I took a step away from him.

"You can see me?" I asked, my soul-shaking with the realization that someone could glimpse me... Someone that shouldn't be able to. "You know my name?"

The man nodded. "I understand it's surprising to you, but I'll explain as quickly as possible. I had a near-death experience, and it left me with... Certain gifts," he said, his dark brows drawing into a frown as his handsome face tensed in concern.

"Who are you?" I asked, tilting my head, curious about the only man who could see me even when I was invisible to everyone, including Shayla.

"My name is Leo Fair," he said as people passed him, gazing at him as if he had lost his mind. I suppose it appeared as if he had because, to them, he was speaking to thin air. He shifted as he gazed toward me, clearly uncomfortable with their stares. Still, he continued. "Shayla is in trouble."

"How do you know?" I asked, frowning as I tilted my head, listening to the thump of her heart. It wasn't the steady thumping of before. Instead, it was galloping, becoming quicker with each beat.

"It's one of those gifts," he said, shaking his head. "Of course, no one really believes me about them, but you will. She's been informed that the lawyer is on his way."

"I'm about to prevent him from doing that," I said, glancing toward the building, determination sliding through me.

Leo shook his head sadly. "By then, it will be too late for her," he said, his voice quivering with worry. "You must go now or the one you wish to protect will no longer need protecting. She has become desperate and with desperation comes her death."

My eyes widened. "You mean she's—"

But I couldn't finish the sentence as Leo simply nodded his head. I didn't thank him. I didn't say anything else to him as my soul trembled and I turned, trying to get to Shayla before she took her life but as I moved closer to her, I heard her heart slow, and I realized her life had already begun to fade.

I ENTERED SHAYLA'S apartment, rushing up the stairs through the door, finding her on the bathroom floor. I fell to my knees beside her, gazing into her face as a sob broke from my throat. I could still hear her heart around me getting weaker and pulling her further away from me, but I had no idea what I should do. How did I save her?

The pounding on the door made my head snap up as I realized that there was a way to help her. I rushed to the door, unlocking it.

Belinda moved into the room, her eyes moving toward the bathroom, widening when she saw Shayla on the floor.

"Jim is going to kill me," she said, her voice shaking, her fear so potent that she didn't even question who unlocked the door.

"Save her," I said into her ear. She jumped as she realized I was in the room with her.

"And how will I do that?" She asked, and then gave a mirthless laugh. "She's as good as dead."

"Call an ambulance," I said, quickly, feeling Shayla slip further away with every word.

Belinda shook her head, but I was done arguing with her as I reached into her chest, taking her heart in my hand. She gasped, her eyes widening in a silent plea.

"Call them now or you will die," I said through clenched teeth.

Belinda nodded, and I pulled my hand away from her heart. She didn't argue further. Instead, she took her phone out of her pocket with shaky hands and dialed.

"If she dies, so do you," I said, angrily, causing her to pale as she continued to talk to the dispatcher, giving her information as quickly as possible.

"P-Please hurry," she said, tears rolling down her face. It angered me that the tears weren't for Shayla but fear for her own survival.

Belinda never did anything that didn't benefit her.

A few minutes later, the ambulance arrived. I watched them as they worked and then followed them to the hospital. Shayla opened her eyes, staring straight into my soul as they pushed the gurney into the hospital.

"Hunter...wanted...to...be...with...you," she said, struggling to speak through the grogginess. "Sorry."

I swallowed because the realization that I was near was hurting her and giving her a reason to end her life. I closed my eyes, knowing I was going to have to fade from her life to give her a chance at a normal one, but first, I would have to kill those who would harm her. I would have to give her freedom from her abusers and from me, so that she could live.

Chapter Thirty/ Shayla

I DIDN'T DIE. I DIDN'T know whether to be thankful or disappointed when my eyes opened in the bright hospital room. Belinda sat next to the bed; her eyes narrowed upon me with a magazine in her lap. I glanced around the room, my gaze settling on Hunter standing beside the door. His eyes were dark as they found mine, and a frown settled on his face.

"Look who's awake," Belinda said, but I refused to acknowledge her. After a few minutes, she grunted and left the room to find a doctor.

"Hunter," I whispered, the pain on his face melting into his eyes as he shook his head, his disappointment clear in the gesture. Shame enveloped me as I shifted on the bed.

"You were going to give up," he whispered, voice angry, but his eyes gave away his pain.

"I don't want this anymore," I whispered, glancing around the room. "I don't want to be tortured every day."

"And I was fixing that," he said, stepping toward me as he took a deep breath. His shoulders bowed forward as he peered at me through his lashes. "But instead, you were going to take the reaper at his word when he wanted you to keep your discussion with him a secret. He enticed you with death. Why would you trust him?" He yelled that last.

I jerked, wishing I could deny it, but the truth was, he had a right to be angry. Both the reaper and I had kept a secret from him, but it appeared he already knew.

"How long have you known?" I asked, my chin quivering as I tried to keep my eyes on him, but the shame... The ever-present shame pushed my eyes to the floor.

"Since right after it happened," he said, his jaws tight as my eyes moved back to him. "I was hoping you would trust me more than him."

"I do trust you, but you don't live this every day," I said, my heart aching. "You don't have to worry about what torture will come next. You don't have to worry about something going wrong. You don't have to face it."

"No, I don't live your life. I don't live at all. My life was taken from me," he said. I flinched. "Which is why I will do my job and I will free you, but you won't see me anymore."

I jerked as if he had slapped me. He was going to leave me... Leave me alone. "You said you loved me," I said, my heart so heavy that it felt as if it would fall from my chest.

"I do," he said, his eyes darkening. His pain swirled within the blue depths. "That's why I'm doing this. I will be near you, but you won't see me. You won't sense me, but you will see that I will do the job to free you."

I shook my head as tears fell down my cheeks. "No, you don't love me," I said, my heart cracking before falling to pieces. A tremble shook through my body. "If you did, you wouldn't be doing this."

Hunter's eyes darkened further. The shimmer of tears rested within their blue depths, but he blinked, and they were gone. "If it helps you to believe that... If it helps you live, then believe it."

Then, he was gone as sobs broke from me, racking through my body and soul.

TWO DAYS PASSED AND Hunter kept his word. I hadn't seen him, nor did I feel him nearby. I was just as alone and miserable as I had been before his arrival. Still, I wouldn't cry. I just laid in the hospital bed motionless while trying to numb myself to the pain moving through me like poison.

"The doctor says you can go home today," Belinda said, gaining my attention. I didn't even know she was still in the room until she had spoken. My stomach churned. I didn't want to return to the home of most of my tortures.

I didn't say anything to her until she raised her brow. "Is ghost boy not around?" She asked, causing me to raise my head to stare at her in disbelief.

"What are you talking about?" I asked, frowning, keeping my face as stoic as possible because there was something dangerous glinting in her eyes.

"Hunter," she said, and I flinched. Even his name caused a chasm of pain deep in my chest. "That's the name you were calling as they brought you into the hospital."

"You've lost your mind," I said, turning away from her, but I heard her rise. It was Jim's voice that stopped her from inflicting whatever pain she had intended.

"What are you doing, Belinda?" He snapped, his voice gruff and full of the promise of danger.

"I'm making sure our little patient is okay for her release," she said, moving back to her chair and sitting down.

Jim moved close to the bed, waiting for a few moments before he sighed. "Shayla, look at me," he said, his voice low enough the medical staff wouldn't be able to eavesdrop. I resisted at first, but he didn't move.

Slowly, I turned, taking in through narrowed eyes the man who took my innocence... The man who ruined me and Desi and Hunter, not caring if he was angry. I only wanted him to go away.

"I pulled some strings," he said, his face stony. "You'll be home today."

"I don't want to go home," I said, raising my chin as I stared into his eyes, daring him to make a scene in the hospital.

He gripped my chin between his fingers, pressing painfully into the skin. "You are going home, and you will not do this again," he said, raising his brow. "And you will be punished for this incident."

I raised my eyes defiantly. "Go ahead... Punish me," I said in challenge. "What can you do that you haven't done already?"

"How about I just make you compliant?" he said, throwing files on my lap.

I opened them as tears sprang to my eyes. There were pictures and addresses of Hunter's family. Desi's picture stared up at me, causing my heart to ache.

"There are worse things than death," Jim said, his nostrils flaring. "Guess who will take your place if you pull a stunt like this again?"

My bottom lip trembled as I met Jim's eyes, hatred like no other flowing through me. "Her parents won't let you hurt her."

Jim smiled, but it was cold and callous. "Her parents are expendable, just like her brother," he said, smiling when a tear escaped my eye. "And guess what? Her birthday is coming up."

A deep breath shuddered from me as my bravery faded. "I won't do anything like this again," I said as a tear fell from my eye, tracking its way down my cheek. "I won't try to die. Just leave her alone."

"That's what I thought," Jim said, smiling in a way that churned my stomach.

I closed my eyes, hoping that Hunter was near and had heard Jim. Even if he was mad at me, he wouldn't let someone hurt Desi. As I stared at the monster before me, I could only hope Hunter would keep his promise and Jim's death would happen soon.

Chapter Thirty-one/ Hunter

I WATCHED HER... MY heart ached the entire time, wishing I could touch her, be with her. Her solemn silence broke me the first day, and I realized I couldn't stay there watching her in pain without breaking. I had to keep my promise to alleviate her of the people who harmed her, but I also had to keep my word that she wouldn't see me because my presence in her life was dangerous, pushing her to the point of taking her life.

She was safe in the hospital the second day. I knew they shouldn't release her after such an attempt on her life until she had gone through the mental evaluation, so I left that morning while she slept, touching her cheek, wincing when I realized that the nightmares had come back in my absence. I gritted my teeth, tearing myself away from her as my soul ached for me to return.

I walked through the streets toward a hotel, following Aaron Cleaveston, determined to rid him from Shayla's life. I gritted my teeth as he opened the door to the hotel room, bracing myself for whatever was beyond it.

A jolt of anger shot through me when I saw a girl, no older than thirteen, sitting on the bed. Tears glistened in her eyes as the man standing beside her gripped her biceps in his meaty hand, causing more tears to fall down her already wet face.

"Where did you find this one, Clay?" Aaron asked, raising his brow as he stared at her, taking her in with a lascivious grin.

"Her mother sold her for her fix," he said, laughing as my lip curled in disgust. How could a mother sell her child? It was sickening.

"The girl begged me the whole way not to do this. She should put up quite a fight."

I glanced at the girl, seeing the innocence in her expression as my stomach churned. I narrowed my eyes at the men, deciding who to take out first, hating that I would frighten the girl further, but I knew it was better than what she would face if I left them alive.

The beefy man beside her chuckled, his eyes glinting with malice. I moved toward him, realizing he was the one who brought the little girls to this man and probably others. He had ruined countless lives. I shook my head.

"You won't be doing anything to her or anyone else again," I said, making sure he was the only one able to hear me. The man stiffened as his eyes widened.

"What the hell?" He asked, glancing around the room in a panic.

"Hell is right," I said, putting my hand through his chest. "What if I bought your daughter, or mother, or your sister? How would that feel?"

Guilt moved through him as he glanced around while grasping his chest. It scented the air and I knew he was ready to meet the reaper. "If there is any justice in the afterlife, hell is where you'll be heading."

I gripped his heart, hard enough the blood pulsed against my hand, fighting to continue its path through his veins and failing, causing him to release the girl, stumbling back until he fell on the bed, gripping his chest, his eyes wide open. His soul glided into me.

"Clay?" Aaron said, his eyes rushing to the man as the girl squealed and stumbled off the bed away from the dead man.

Aaron stepped toward him; his brows furrowed as he felt for a pulse.

"Damn it," he whispered, glancing at the girl who had moved to the far side of the room, shaking as her eyes shifted away from the man who would be her tormentor. His eyes flashed as he gazed at her.

"Now, what the hell am I going to do with you?"

"Nothing. You won't touch any other child... Not her... Not your daughter... No other child will be subject to your evil," I said, my nostrils flaring as I reached into his chest and squeezed. I could feel his guilt as images of his wife and daughter flashed through his mind. Shame slid through him as he realized they would know of his dark deeds. His eyes widened as he grasped his chest, his face red.

He fell in a heap at my feet. The girl sobbed as she glanced around, as if waiting for something to happen to her.

"It's okay," I said, softly. "No harm will come to you, but you need to leave. Don't go back to your mother. She'll just sell you again."

The girl nodded as she glanced around the room, still searching for me. Her lips trembled as she opened the door before glancing back once more.

"Thank you... Whoever you are," she said, and then she was gone.

I glanced at the two men on the floor, wondering how long it would be before their deaths made it back to Shayla. I could only hope that it would bring her some kind of solace and take away the awful, empty look in her eyes that my absence had caused.

I LISTENED TO THE STEADY beating of Shayla's heart gaining peace from the fact that she was still alive even when I wasn't with her. Still, I missed her. My soul ached with the absence of her, and I had to remind myself that I was doing this for her to have a normal life.

"She'll never have a normal life," a man said behind me, reading my mind. I frowned as I turned, finding Leo standing on the sidewalk, his face grim as he faced me. I didn't ask how he had found me. I knew it was one of his many gifts.

"What do you mean?" I asked, stepping closer to him, my brows furrowed as I met his dark eyes.

A familiar sorrow blanketed his face. "She's been marked by her life and that will follow her to her death. You can't stop that." I sighed, my soul heavy, knowing he was right. "I have to try."

Leo swallowed, his gaze darkening even more. "You don't understand... Her life will be too short for that."

"Too short?" I asked, tilting my head as I listened to her heartbeat thrum.

His silence stretched as my soul pulsed with desperation. I wouldn't allow her to die. She deserved a life... A real life of peace and love. Still, her heart drummed on.

"She's alive," I said, his words causing me to panic. "She still lives and as long as she lives, there's a chance. I've stopped her torture. I can stop anyone who harms her."

Leo shook his head, his face drawn. "Minutes ago, it was decided her life would end," he said, grief blanketing his features. "You won't make it back before her murderer reaches her."

I shook my head, "You're wrong," I called over my shoulder, as I ran toward the center of town, her heartbeat still pulsing in my ears.

Panic and fear fueled me as my soul shuddered, aching with the thought of Shayla's death... The thought that she would die believing I didn't love her still fresh in her mind. The reaper's promise meant little to me because I wasn't sure he told the truth. If he wasn't truthful, I would never see her again.

Light bulbs burst above me as the energy from them came to me unbidden. Cars that were moving past me lost all power, leaving their drivers stranded, but I didn't stop running. I had to reach her.

"Please," I whispered repeatedly to whatever god was listening as I rushed closer and closer.

Her heart picked up speed as I crossed over to her side of town.

Homes pulsed with power and then fell to darkness as I continued. Dread settled into my soul as Leo's warning echoed in my ears.

I turned down her street, determined to arrive at her apartment before her death. Her heartbeat was still thumping wildly in my ears, pushing me forward until I reached her door but as I stepped over the threshold, the erratic thumping stopped, and I was met with only the terrifying silence that told me I had lost the only woman I had ever loved.

Chapter Thirty-Two/
Shayla

I ALWAYS KNEW IT WOULD be Belinda who would ultimately end my life. Jim was a threat... Yes, but where he was led by lust and power, Belinda was led by vengeance and hatred. That potent combination ticked like a bomb waiting to go off and, when it did, I would be the victim caught in her final display of revenge.

After returning from the hospital, I tried to sleep but instead I stared at the door, almost as if I knew deep down, tonight would be the night she came for me... Tonight would be the night she would finally destroy my life. Perhaps there was a tingling in my consciousness warning me to cherish each breath, but instead, I simply waited for the end.

I suppose most would believe that she wouldn't do such a thing when she had saved my life less than two days before until they took into consideration, she did it for her own survival. Either way, when the lock released on my door and she entered holding a knife gripped in her fist, I wasn't surprised to find her there. Instead, I wondered what had taken her so long.

"You're awake," she said, surprised to find me staring at her with a mixture of apathy and relief. At least Hunter wouldn't blame me for taking my life this time. I raised my brows because for the first time in years, her voice was not slurring with the alcohol she loved so much. She was completely lucid.

"And you're sober," I whispered, but my voice was steady. It was odd not to be frightened with my death so close when I had been frightened for most of my life. There was a weird acceptance of what was about to happen. I was... Calm.

"It's kind of hard to be drunk when you can't tell which bottle has been poisoned," she said, her lip curling into a sneer while her eyes swept around the room as if waiting for retribution.

"It sucks not to be able to do something as simple as eating without worrying you're going to be sick, doesn't it?" I asked, moving to stand because if she was going to kill me, she would have to do so facing me and I was going to go down while standing on my feet.

She regarded me with suspicion, her eyes flashing with fear. "Why are you so calm?" She asked, frowning, "Is he here?"

"Who?" I asked, not because I was denying Hunter's existence but because I wanted to hear her say his name... To acknowledge he was real. I wanted her to feel as uncomfortable as I had felt my whole life.

"Hunter... Hunter De Haven," she said, causing a slight smile to move across my lips. "The boy Jim killed."

I stared at her, deciding the truth would probably make her more nervous than a lie. "I have no idea."

"You're lying," she said, taking a step toward me, pointing the knife at my chest. "You do have an idea. You can see him."

"Usually, but sometimes, like now, he's even hidden from me," I said, my heart aching with that fact. "He may be hidden from me for eternity."

"He abandoned you... Like everyone else?" She asked, taking a step closer, sighing with relief when nothing happened.

"My mother didn't abandon me," I said, narrowing my eyes. "You hired someone to kill her."

Belinda flinched. "He told you... Huh?"

"But it didn't quench that need for revenge, did it?" I asked, raising my brows. "Especially when you realized my dad would never love you like he had loved her. Then you killed him with your selfishness."

"I didn't kill him," she said through clenched teeth. Her control over her emotions was slipping.

"Maybe not directly, but you did tempt him with the very thing that ended his life," I said, raising my chin. "He was trying to quit drinking and wanted to stop getting high and you couldn't have that because he would see how truly awful you were without the haze of alcohol and drugs. You refused to become a better person and realized he would leave you when he witnessed who you truly are."

"I loved him!" She shouted, but I didn't even flinch.

"That's not love... It's lust and greed and selfishness," I said with a mirthless laugh. "I don't think you have any idea what love is. If you truly loved my father, you would have sacrificed your own feelings for him to be happy. You would have let him go but instead, you killed his wife, trapped him, and hurt his daughter even after his death, but don't worry... He knows all your sins now. Any affection he may have had for you in life faded the moment he died."

She trembled as she glanced around the room, faltering for a moment, probably terrified that my father had joined Hunter to torment her. "That's not true."

"I only want you to tell me one thing before you do this final sin... And it will be a final sin because I don't see you living long afterwards," I said, staring into her eyes. "Why torture me... Why sell me and beat me and find ways to make my life hell? I did nothing to you."

Belinda's lips curled, becoming a cruel smile. "Because you were hers," she said, simply. "That's the only reason. I wanted to punish you for being born her daughter and being a reminder of her every single day. With you around, I could never have what I wanted."

"It was always about you... Never Dad, or anyone else," I said, narrowing my eyes. "Whatever Hunter did to you, you deserved and while you lay dying, know you deserved that too... and whatever tortures happen after your death, you earned every single bit of it."

I understood she had reached her limit as a scream emitted from her and she moved toward me. I punched her, refusing to die without fighting. At least in this, Hunter could be proud of me. Her nose cracked beneath my knuckles as I punched again and again.

She staggered backwards, but her grip on the knife tightened as she delivered her first blow. Hot pain spread down my abdomen, and I glanced down, watching as a crimson stain spread over my white shirt. She didn't wait for me to recover as she raised the knife again, hitting me in the shoulder and knocking me down. She straddled my body and raised the knife over her head before arching it downward into my chest... This one bringing darkness and death as my heart ceased beating with Hunter's face, the last conscious image in my mind.

A BRIGHT LIGHT FLASHED before me, becoming brighter and brighter. A hand gripped mine, but it was too bright to see the owner. Then, the voice came, bringing up memories of a childhood that would have been wonderful if the owner of that hand had continued to live.

I stared into emerald eyes that matched my own, taking in her beautiful, familiar face.

"You'll wait with me in the veil until the reaper comes for you," she said softly as she embraced me. The scent of cookies baking in the oven, and flower chains brought back those sepia tinted memories of the past, and with it, I was finally brought to peace in the presence of my mother.

Chapter Thirty-Three/
Hunter

I CLOSED MY EYES, MY soul shaking as I slipped through the apartment, glancing toward the kitchen. Bottles upon bottles of liquor and wine were turned upside down in the sink. I realized Belinda had been busy getting rid of the alcohol she believed to be poisoned. Her fear still hung in the room as rancid as the alcohol coating the air.

I stepped toward the stairs with Shayla's heart still silent as I moved onto the landing. I gazed at the door to her room, terrified of what I would find beyond it. Hesitating, I stepped into the room, the metallic scent of blood assaulting me. My eyes moved over the room, stopping on the body of the woman I loved. Her eyes were facing me; the sparkle of life gone from them, replaced with the dull look of death. Belinda sat beside her on the floor, breathing harshly and gripping the knife, still slick with Shayla's blood in her hands. Speckles of crimson dotted her face.

Laughter broke from her, demented but broken, as blood dripped off her chin onto the white shirt now dyed a sickening red. My heart twisted as I realized Shayla had fought Belinda and I wasn't there for her. I had left her abandoned and unprotected. The promises I had made sliced through the air, falling around me. Dead like Shayla.

My eyes settled on Belinda, anger sliding through me as I moved toward her. The room became abnormally cold. Her breaths puffed in front of her, and she glanced around, searching for a sign that I was there.

"It's too late," she said, cackling as she held her stomach. "I've killed her. You can't bring her back."

"No," I said, my nostrils flaring at the woman I hated more than any other because she had snuffed out the life of the woman I loved. "But I can make sure you die and die painfully."

She laughed again, but it was mirthless and cruel. "No matter what you do to me, I still win," she said, twisting the knife in her hands. "She's still dead and gone, and you'll never see her again."

The reaper's promise whispered through my mind. I had to hope he spoke the truth. I winced because whether he told the truth or not may not matter. After what I had done, Shayla may not want to join me. The pain of that tore through me. I glanced at this evil woman sitting beside Shayla, not wanting her near her.

I reached forward, all the pain and anger twisting through me as I picked her up by the neck. Her feet hovered a foot above the floor as a shriek of fear broke from her and washed over me... Through me as her sins played out in my mind. I witnessed everything Shayla had said... Everything she had done before her demise and though I felt pride, it only made the grief worse.

"I hope there is a hell," I growled as I stared into her too-wide eyes as she struggled for breath. "I hope you face everything you did to her, her father and her mother. For now, you will be going to the reaper."

My soul flickered as her eyes widened. Every sin she had done pulsed through her... burned through her. Her mouth opened as she trembled.

"That is a preview of what you'll face in the afterlife," I growled through my teeth. "Every demon there is waiting for you."

I gripped her hand, still holding the knife, and forced her hand back to bury the knife in her chest. A gasp slid from her mouth as blood bubbled on her lips. With her last spark of life, I could see a moment of her torment in the afterlife. I sneered cruelly at her as her eyes lost all life and I dropped her to my feet on the floor. I went to Shayla's body, falling to my knees beside her. I took her hand. Even in death, I could feel the coolness there rapidly taking any warmth she had. I held her hand and gave my soul over to a grief so immense it began to rip my sanity apart.

THE LIGHT OF THE REAPER washed over me, and I snapped my head up to look at him. His robes blew around him as if a gentle wind was brushing over him. His shoulders were bent as if broken in his own grief.

"You promised her we would be together," I said, my voice broken as I stared at him, ready to beg for a chance to see her again... To hold her and tell her I love her. I was willing to do anything, even spend time in the horrid prison of the afterlife I had glimpsed in Belinda's eyes as she died.

The reaper tilted his head. "I did," he whispered, hesitating. "And I have been called for her soul, but it will be her choice to return to you."

Tears fell down my face. "Why did you make the promise to her when you knew it would entice her with death?" I asked, choking over the words as I tried to determine whether he was a friend or someone who wished to cause us pain.

"It wasn't to entice her with death," he said softly. "I knew how close she was coming to her own demise. I gave her the promise to bring her peace when it happened."

"I was protecting her," I whispered, but as I looked down at her body, I realized I was always doomed to fail.

"And you would have continued to try, but her name has shown up in our books many times. Though Belinda, or whichever of the many others who thought to kill her, always changed their minds, I knew that someone who consistently shows up in our books will eventually have their name written permanently in them," the reaper said, softly, his voice drenched in the sadness of Shayla's death.

My soul ached as I turned to him, finally understanding that he meant no harm. "You shouldn't have kept it from me," I said, softly.

"I agree," the reaper said, his shoulders bowing further forward. "And I have learned from that mistake. I will not keep anything from you any longer. I simply ask for some time to find out Shayla's answer before I reveal all to you."

I nodded as the door to the room opened and Jim came in, taking in Belinda's body before his eyes settled on Shayla. His lip curled in disgust as he turned to his bodyguard, who had entered the room with him.

"It looks like Belinda killed her and then killed herself," the man said, shaking his head.

"That fucking bitch," Jim said, glaring at Belinda's body. "She was always too much trouble and now, she's cost me money. It will take years to train another girl like Shayla."

"Do you want me to call the police to clean up this mess?" The bodyguard asked.

"No, Vaughn," Jim said, shaking his head. "People knew Shayla as my goddaughter. I don't need the press. Dump them in the ocean and get our associates to clean up the blood. I'll tell people they left town for Shayla's mental well-being."

I stared at Jim with narrowed eyes, wanting to kill him, but the reaper stopped me. "His time will come, and it will come at Shayla's hands, not yours," he said, softly. "Let him bury her with you. Allow him to live for now, but when the time comes, I'll let you witness the final blow."

"What do I do until then?" I asked, angry that Jim would walk away unscathed, even if for a little while.

"Wait until my return," the reaper said, his voice gentle. "And hope that Shayla decides to come back to you. Either way, I will come back with answers to your questions."

My soul trembled as I nodded, but he vanished, leaving me in the dark, waiting to find out if the soul of the woman I loved would return to me or if she would decide that her heart and soul were no longer mine.

Chapter Thirty-Four/
Shayla

THE LIGHT FADED FROM around me and, for the first time since I was a child; I looked upon my mother's beautiful face. The dark hair that I had always loved so much billowed around her, complementing her porcelain skin. Tears slid down my cheeks as she smiled, her eyes dark with sadness, but still, she looked like an angel.

"My beautiful Shayla," she said, cupping my cheek gently in her delicate hands. "I'm so proud of you."

I shook my head, my soul aching as my shame engulfed me. Everything I had been forced to do had sullied me. I shifted. My mother should be disgusted and disappointed, not proud. "How can you be? I've been made to do a lot of awful things."

My mother's smile faltered as she shook her head. "Shayla, that shame should be placed on the people who did those things to you," she said, her eyes shining. "That shame isn't yours to bear. You should be proud because you're strong... Much stronger than they are."

A shudder shook through me as I tried to grasp onto her words... To believe them. I tried, but I couldn't push away all those emotions that had swamped me most of my life. "I-I didn't fight," I sobbed. "I didn't fight them."

"You did what you needed to do to survive," she said, softly, caressing my face. "That is still fighting."

Survive... The moment of desperation where I wanted my heart to cease beating drifted through my mind. I didn't try to fight then. I didn't try to survive and had lost the man I loved because of it.

"I tried to take my life," I whispered, the words flowing over trembling lips. "H-Hunter, he left me. He doesn't love me anymore because I was weak... Because I tried to give up."

My mother sighed. "He does love you, Shayla," she said, her voice almost a whisper as she kissed my forehead. Images swamped my mind. I saw the heartbreak of him finding my body, the anger of Belinda's taunts leading to her death before he fell to his knees and then begged the reaper for my return. His voice was desperate as his emotions ran through me, so potent and so tragic that I almost fell to my knees. Warmth moved through me as I felt his love, so pure... So light that I gasped as it wrapped around my soul.

My mother pulled away from me, staring into my eyes. "You see now," she said, a smile lifting her lips.

I nodded, my soul aching as the reaper appeared beside me. I stared at my mother with wide eyes as the consequences of my return to him hit my soul, damaging it further. To join Hunter meant I left my mother.

Her hand moved over my cheek as her eyes sparkled with understanding. "Shayla, I'm not ready for you to be here," she said as if she had read my mind. "You haven't found happiness and I need for you to do that before you come back to me. When it is time, I will meet you and Hunter here together."

My soul ached. "I miss you," I whispered as she pulled me into her arms. "I miss you so much."

"And I miss you but I'm always there with you," she said as she kissed my forehead again but this time, her emotions slid through me... Peace... Happiness... Love... So much love that it made it easier for me to decide.

I nodded as I backed away from her and she faded from me, but this time, there was peace with her absence. This time the grief was only a dull ache that would always be there when we were apart, but it was one that didn't rip my soul in two every time I thought of her. Instead, where there was once turmoil, there was now peace.

I TURNED TO THE REAPER. His robes billowed around him as the sadness of my death bowed his shoulders. A heavy sigh broke from beneath his hood, washing over me as I wondered at his grief. He didn't know me... He had only met me once, but I sensed his deep sadness.

"So, you will go back to Hunter?" He asked, his voice a little lighter than his grief.

"I will," I said as the reaper breathed out slowly.

"That relieves me more than you know." He stepped closer to me. I nodded. "What will happen to Belinda's soul?"

The reaper's robes twitched. "I've already delivered it to a place where the rest of her punishment will be given," he said, his voice heavy.

"Where is that place?" I asked, hoping to get an idea of what the afterlife held for those who were punished and those who were not.

"Some call it hell," he said, his voice soft. "Others call it Tartarus. Others call it something else, but it remains the same. A place where punishment is given to those who have hurt and killed. "Why do you ask?"

I paused, trying to make sense of my emotions. "Though I feel punishment is what she deserves, there is sadness there," I said, my soul aching. "But it's because she could have been a better person. She might have been kinder and chosen not to do these things. Instead, she chose to hurt everyone she met."

"You're sad for a life wasted on sins," he said, his hood bowing, as if to nod. "I do understand that." he was silent for a moment before he continued. "There are no winners in justice. The victim has already been harmed and the punishment only validates them. It doesn't take away the pain caused. I think you understand that the pain done to you will not go away simply because justice has been served. That is something you must heal from on your own."

"I think it's too late for me," I said, as the immense sadness of my life wrapped around me. "How can I heal when I'm dead?"

The reaper turned to me. "The death of your body doesn't stop you from healing," he said softly. "Besides, the injuries you have left are injuries of your soul. That is something that still pulses with life long after your death."

I nodded, melancholy deepening within me. "I guess I still wish I was able to live a life... A mortal life with Hunter, where we could have dated and gotten married and maybe even had children."

He smiled as he lifted his head and, for the first time, I saw his face. His eyes shined with kindness and joy as he took my hand in his.

"What if I told you that could happen?" He asked, his eyes sparkling. "What if I told you that you can still have that life with Hunter and you both could live?"

My soul trembled. "But we're dead," I said, but even as I spoke those words, hope sprung to life.

"For now," the reaper said, his voice light. "I want to take you back to Hunter now, but I can explain when you're together."

I nodded as that hope brightened inside of me. If he could truly give us back our lives, then I would allow him to explain anything he wanted.

Chapter Thirty-Five/ Hunter

I WAS GOING INSANE with the wait. Hours passed as I watched Jim's men come and clean the room before leaving me alone in the dark. I sat on Shayla's bed, staring at all her possessions, grief sweeping through me as I admonished myself for leaving her alone. My mind would never let me forget that she died thinking I didn't love her. I shoved my hands through my hair, allowing bitter tears to fall down my cheeks while begging silently for her return, but as each second ticked by; I lost more and more hope.

I got up and paced through my nervous energy while I waited. I'd absorbed so much energy coming here, that it was hard to sit still. The anticipation of the reaper's return made it even harder. The tension built, and I couldn't stay in this room with my love's body lying on the floor. I would wait somewhere else. The reaper would find me. As I started through the door, light spread through the room, and I turned, blinded but refusing to look away. My soul leapt as I took in Shayla's face. The shock that she had chosen to return to me tore through me and a sob broke from my throat.

I stood there, waiting for her judgment, waiting for her to condemn me for abandoning her. Instead, she moved toward me, pulling me into her arms. I savored the feel of her beneath my hands as I kissed her forehead, her eyes and her cheeks before pressing my lips against hers.

She wrapped her arms around me, pulling me closer. Tears continued to flow down my face... Tears of relief... Tears of remorse that

I hadn't been there for her... Tears because she died thinking I didn't love her... Tears because she chose to be with me.

I pulled away from the kiss but couldn't release her as I peered into her eyes. "I love you," I said, hoping she would believe me... Hoping she would forgive me.

"I love you too," she whispered, cupping my cheek as she stared into my eyes. "Why are you crying?"

My face twisted in remorse as I stumbled over my words. "I-I thought I'd lost you."

She shook her head. "No, Hunter," she whispered, her voice gentle as a smile slid across her face. "You will never lose me."

"I waited so long," I whispered, my lips trembling over the words.

"I was visiting my mother," she said, her eyes shining with more peace than I had ever seen within them. "And then, the reaper came, and we spoke for a while."

I blinked, turning toward the reaper. I had forgotten he was in the room with us.

"What did you talk about?" I asked, frowning.

"Don't worry. I'll tell you," He said. His voice had lost that raspy quality, sounding vaguely familiar. I frowned, trying to place where I had heard it before. "But first—."

He removed his hood and my eyes widened as I stared into the face of the only other mortal who could see me while in my ghost form.

I blinked, confusion sweeping through me as I took in his face. "Leo?"

"I realize some explanation is needed," Leo said, his brown eyes darkening as he glanced from me to Shayla.

"How can you be a reaper if you are human?" I asked, wondering if I was wrong, but I couldn't be. He walked among the living. They could see him. I noticed that each time he spoke to me and those around him would stare.

"I'll explain all of it, but I'd like to tell you who I am first," he said, shifting beneath his robes.

"That would be best," Shayla said, glancing at me as she gripped my hand harder within hers, giving me comfort with that small action.

The reaper nodded. "My name is Leo Fair," he said, softly. "I was born in the Summer of 1835 to a slave mother and father in Georgia."

"That's too much time to have passed for you to be alive. So, you aren't mortal?" I asked, as Shayla's eyes widened.

"I am, but I'm not. I will get to that," Leo said, his body shifting again.

"I was sold. I don't know my parent's names. I have little memory of them," he said, his brow furrowing. "I worked for the Fair family in Georgia. Their daughter, Mary Beth, was the most beautiful person I had ever laid eyes on. When I was seventeen, I was injured in the fields and she found me, healing me with the medicine she made. During that time, we fell in love. When she became pregnant, I understood it was a death sentence for me. We tried to run, but her father found us. I was hung and Mary Beth was taken somewhere to have the baby. The midwife was supposed to kill our child, but she didn't. Instead, she told Mary Beth's father he was stillborn. The midwife raised him with frequent visits from Mary Beth. Though our relationship was very much like yours was, she was forced into marriage to a white man who eventually found out her secret and beat her to death."

Silent tears fell down Shayla's face. "I'm so sorry."

"It's no fault of yours, Shayla," Leo said, giving her a smile. "Upon my death, a reaper gave me the same deal I gave Hunter. He was a man who had been murdered sometime in the 1700s. When Mary Beth was killed, a new deal came into place."

"A new deal?" I asked, frowning.

"My reaper, Bartholomeus, saw the growing evil in the world. He wanted to grow the number of reapers with hopes of balancing the scales. Mary Beth and I continued his work, helping him find those who deserve justice like you and Shayla and in return we would live again. We want you both to join us," Leo said, pausing before taking a deep breath. "You will be given the same powers we have. We'll teach you to use them and you will be given life."

"We're dead," Shayla said, shaking her head. "There are people who know we're dead."

"Not the right people," Leo said, grinning. "Your bodies were dumped in the ocean. No one has found you and no one will. You are just as alive on paper as you've always been."

"My family?" Hunter asked, hope filling his eyes.

"You'll be able to see them and have a relationship with them. You can get married and have children," Leo said, sighing. "Of course, eventually they will have to know your secret, or you'll have to leave them. In most cases, family is very accepting. The midwife and my son certainly were. However, your long life means you'll outlive them. You must be prepared for that."

I wanted to accept as soon as he said the words, but my gaze moved to Shayla, whose brow was furrowed.

"We still have to kill those who have done evil," she said, her eyes meeting Leo's. "How do we do that without getting caught?"

"Your soul travels," Leo said, motioning to himself. "My soul is here, but my body is not. A soul killing someone is the same as a ghost. You won't get caught."

"And you'll show us how to do this?" she asked, softly.

"You'll live with Mary Beth and I," he said, grinning. "You'll work in our business. You'll have a normal human life apart from the reaping. I promise."

Shayla turned to me, her smile returning to her face. "I want to live with you. I want a life with you."

I pulled her close to me, kissing her forehead. "I do too."

Shayla turned to Leo and nodded. "Then, we accept."

Leo smiled and stepped forward, placing his hands on each of our heads. "When you wake, your bodies will be as alive as your souls. I'll meet you on the beach with my wife."

Light blinded me and I closed my eyes, falling into a deep sleep. When I woke, I would once again be alive and my life with Shayla would truly begin.

Chapter Thirty-six/
Shayla

I WAS FLOATING IN THE water as my senses came back to me, pulling me up among its dark depths, breaking the surface a moment later. I inhaled sharply, breathing in the air in great gulps as the water flowed over me, pushing me to the beach before landing beside Hunter on the sandy shore, staring at a sky dotted with millions of stars.

I blinked the salty water from my stinging eyes, sitting up to take in Hunter's beautiful face, healed from his time in the sea... Healed from every injury given to him.

Water droplets rested on his face and eyes. As my gaze traveled downward, I became mesmerized by his steadily moving chest as his breaths moved in and out of his mouth. My heart jumped seeing the proof that he was alive.

Slowly, I reached forward, my fingers skimming over his wet cheek. His eyes burst open as he took a deep breath. His hand found mine, rubbing over the skin slick with the ocean water.

"Shayla," he whispered, opening his eyes before a joyous grin spread over his face and he pulled me against him, kissing me. We pulled apart, laughing. I rested my head against his chest, listening to the steady thump of his heart.

The thrill of us both being alive filled me.

"There is another thing to be happy about," he said as I lifted my face to peer into his eyes. "You're free. You don't have to worry about the bidders or Jim anymore."

"Well, that's not exactly true," Leo said, staring down at us with amusement. "Their souls must be reaped."

Hunter frowned. "But she won't be forced to be with them anymore."

"No," Leo said with a smile. "She won't and eventually, you both will be able to live without worry of those who know of your death because those who have harmed you will be gone."

I sighed, realizing I only had one more hurdle to jump and then my old life would be a bad memory. Someone called out to Leo and my gaze Turned toward the owner of the voice. A woman with long brown hair pulled back into a bun moved toward us. She was beautiful, with bright blue eyes and delicate features. She stood beside Leo, a smile sliding over her face.

"I remember the moment we woke up," she said, tilting her head as she studied us. "This is the moment where you are most thankful to be alive."

Leo slid his arm around the woman's waist and placed a delicate kiss on her temple. "You're right. It is," Leo said, turning back to us. "I would like to introduce you to my lovely wife, Mary Beth."

We sat up, still in each other's arms. "It's nice to meet you. My name is Shayla Bell," I said, staring at the woman before me in wonder.

"I'm Hunter De Haven," Hunter said beside me, pulling me closer to him.

She held up a bag with a smile. "I brought some clothes for you," she said, glancing down at the wet, torn clothes we wore. I winced when I realized they were the very same clothes we had died in.

"The outdoor showers should be sufficient to change in," she said, handing me a bag of toiletries, wrinkling her nose. "And hopefully wash off some of the scent of the sea."

I giggled because neither Hunter nor I had noticed the smell. We were too distracted by simply being alive. We made our way to the showers, cleaning away the proof of our burials, but as I washed, I realized there were no cuts, no scars left from Belinda's attack.

I stepped out of the stall, fully dressed, as I met Leo's eyes. "I don't have any scars," I said, frowning.

Leo shook his head. "And neither will Hunter. Your bodies are completely healed. Every injury was wiped from them. There is no evidence that Jim, Belinda, or the men who touched you ever harmed you apart from your hair, but you can dye that back to your natural color when you are ready. So, the only injuries you still suffer are of your soul and mind."

A tear fell down my cheek as I remembered our conversation in the veil. "And those will heal in time."

He nodded as Hunter joined me in a t-shirt, jeans and chucks, running his hand through his dark hair shaking it dry. He came over to me and took my hand.

"Okay, Leo," he said, a grin sliding over his face. "Take us to our new home."

"Once there, we will have much to discuss," Leo said, leading us away from the beach where our first kiss, our burials and our revival happened to face our lives as reapers.

LEO LIVED ON THE OUTSKIRTS of town in a large farmhouse. The yard was lined with beds of flowers, which swayed lightly in the breeze. As we stepped inside our new home, we were led to an office. My eyes widened as I took in pictures of me, and other girls pinned to cork boards on the wall.

"I suppose we can take your picture down now," Leo said, his eyes holding the sadness of my past. "I'm sorry we weren't able to help you sooner."

"You're forgiven," I whispered as my eyes moved to a picture of Desi. I paused, remembering Jim's threat in the hospital. I turned to Leo, who nodded his head sadly.

"She's Jim's new target," he said, putting his hand out to stop Hunter before he could become agitated. "We've already moved your parents to one of our houses. They know we are friends. We promised you would visit them soon and I suggest you do that. Your mother is worried."

Hunter nodded, but his face was still red in anger. "We can't leave Jim to continue to do this to people," Hunter said through clenched teeth.

"And we won't," Leo said, frowning, "But first we must train you. After that, we promise Jim Harris will die."

Every abuse he had ever given me floated through my mind as I raised my head to peer into their eyes. "I have a request."

Leo frowned, his voice hesitant. "What is that?"

"That I'm the one who will give the final blow," I said, waiting for them to deny me, but instead, they all nodded.

Leo's face was grim as he spoke. "We had already decided that. Jim's death will be reaped by you. That's a fitting punishment for a man such as him."

I stared at the picture of Desi. Most would have believed I wanted justice for myself, and I did, but more than that, I wanted justice for Desi. I wanted justice for everyone who felt powerless and faced the kind of life I'd had, and I wanted justice for whoever wondered if death would be easier than facing life because of those who abused them. Maybe then, the world would truly be balanced and there would finally be peace.

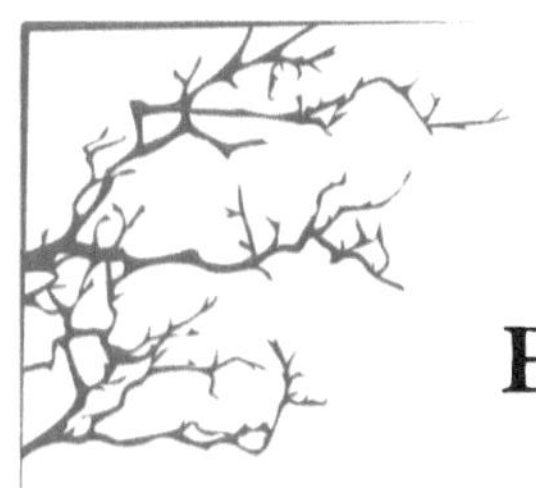

Epilogue/Shayla

WE DROVE FOR TWO HOURS before we stopped in front of a simple but pretty house with white siding. There were no neighbors nearby. The whole place had a sense of tranquility. Hunter's hand was warm in mine. His grip tightened as he pulled into the driveway.

"Ow!" I said, raising my brow. He winced as he released my hand.

"Sorry," he said, his cheeks turning pink.

"I thought I would be the nervous one since I'm the one meeting the parents," I said, tucking a still blonde strand of hair behind my ear.

"They'll love you," he whispered, staring at the house. "You have nothing to be nervous about. I haven't spoken to them in months. My mother won't forgive me so easily."

"I think she will," I said, giving him a smile I hoped would comfort him. He frowned and shook his head.

The front door to the house opened and my eyes widened as I took in the girl before me. Desi had grown, showing the first signs of being a woman, but I could still see the little girl she once was.

Hunter exited the car and walked around to open my door. Desi's eyes were on her brother, filling with tears as she ran to wrap him in her embrace.

"Hunter, where were you?" she asked, her voice trembling. "I was so afraid when you didn't get in touch with us."

"It's okay," Hunter said, trying to blink away the tears resting in his eyes. "I'm here now."

Desi stepped away from him, her eyes turning to me before widening.

"Shayla," she whispered, moving from him to throw herself in my arms.

Tears flowed down my cheeks as she peered up at me. "Did you get away from the mayor?"

"Yeah... He doesn't know where I am now," I said, my voice trembling with emotion.

"What happened to your hair?" She asked, her brows raising.

"Don't worry," I said, tucking a strand behind my ears. "I'm going to dye it back soon."

The door opened again, and Hunter's parents stepped outside the door. His mother stopped as she took in her son's face before running to him, but before embracing him, she slapped his chest.

"You had me scared to death!" She said, glaring at him before hugging him.

"I'm sorry, Ma," he said as his mother gazed at him with narrowed eyes.

"You should be," she said, her voice thick with emotion. When she turned to me, her eyes widened.

"You look familiar," she said, a frown sliding over her face as she tried to place me.

"She's my friend Shayla," Desi said, smiling.

Hunter stared at his mother sheepishly. "She went by her middle name when she met us the first time... Ellie."

His mother's eyes met mine as a grin slid over her face. "So, he finally found you."

Hunter's cheeks flushed crimson. "Ma!"

"I'm just saying. It took you long enough," she said as his father ushered me toward the door.

"They'll be at this for a while," His father said, shaking his head.

"So, now that you found her, what are you going to do?" His mother asked loud enough for me to hear.

Just as I walked over the threshold of the house, his answer drifted toward me, warming my heart. "I'm going to marry her."

I smiled. Though the past would never be erased, I finally had hope for my future. As reapers, I realized that there would be many other people we could give a life to that was worth living and, maybe in that, we could brighten the world for those who were hurt, abused, and lost and perhaps make the past that would always haunt us, fade into our memories.

Dear Readers,

I want to give hope to those who are facing the horrendous things mentioned in this book. Below are some numbers that I hope will help someone who is facing the darkness.

National Suicide Prevention Lifeline: 1-800-273-8255

National Human Trafficking Hotline: 1-888-373-7888

National Domestic Violence Hotline 1-800-799-7233

National Sexual Assault Hotline 1-800-656 4673

National Child Abuse Hotline 1-800-422-4453

With Love,

Amanda

About the Author

Amanda Penn was born in Tullahoma, Tennessee but now lives in Texas. She is the mother of three children, Constance, Izzie and Josh and the grandmother of Maggie and Slade. She is a multi-genre author who has been a published writer since 2012.

www.ingramcontent.com/pod-product-compliance
Lightning Source LLC
Chambersburg PA
CBHW061449150726

47987CB00001B/381